PLAINS OF UTOPIA

COLONY SIX MARS

GERALD M. KILBY

OUTER PLANET
MEDIA

For notifications on upcoming books, and access to my FREE starter library, please join my Readers Group at www.geraldmkilby.com.

CONTENTS

Maps for Print   v

1. Jann   1
2. Nills   8
3. Mia   17
4. Gizmo   25
5. All Wired Up   33
6. Our Sol Will Fall   40
7. The Brandon Waystation   48
8. The Order of Xenon   55
9. Plains of Utopia   62
10. By the Book   68
11. Enclave   75
12. Time to Dig   85
13. Walkabout   92
14. A Promise   104
15. Innermost Cavern   109
16. Primary Directive   116
17. Access Denied   121
18. Shoulder to Shoulder   129
19. Decision Fork   136
20. A Friend in Need   144
21. Failure to Comply   154
22. Network Node   163
23. Atmosphere Processing   172
24. Time to Get Real   181
25. Deserted   187
26. Breakdown   192
27. APU   198
    Epilogue   208

Also by Gerald M. Kilby   217

About the Author   219

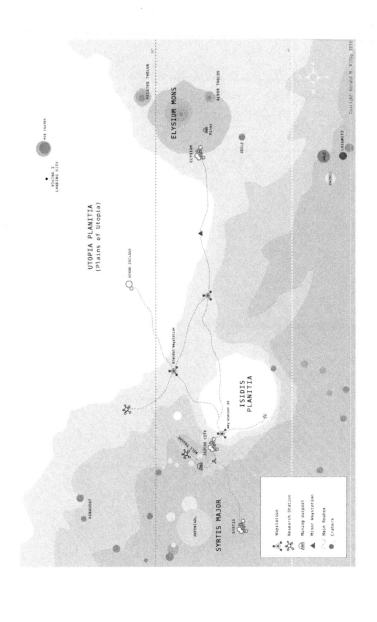

MIE CRATER

VIKING 2
LANDING SITE

UTOPIA PLANITIA
(Plains of Utopia)

VEGETES THOLUS

ELYSIUM MONS

ALBOR THOLUS

HEPHA

ELYSIUM

EDDIE

XENON ENCLAVE

Breuben Waystation

HEMAUGST

Hwy-Station 29

ISIDIS
PLANITIA

KHONEI

GALE

GLASSHITZ

SYRTIS MAJOR

ANTONIADI

JEZERO CITY

WALT TRANAK

SYRTIS

	Waystation
	Research Station
	Mining outpost
	Minor Waystation
	Main Routes
	Craters

Copyright Gerald W. Kitty, 2020

1

JANN

D r. Jann Malbec studied the DNA analysis displayed on screen as Dr. Lewis Dendryte, Head of Forensics, pointed out the salient details—not that he needed to, because it only took Jann a moment to realize there was only one person on Mars with a DNA signature even remotely like the one she was now looking at.

But it was not so much the scientific detail that concerned her, it was more the seismic repercussions. If what she was seeing were true, and she had no reason to doubt it, then something very weird was going on, something that brought back memories of the horrors of an earlier time—a time that Dr. Jann Malbec wished never to experience ever again.

The colony had just come through a yearlong dust storm, further exacerbated by a tech embargo from Earth and a quasi-revolution in Syrtis. The entire period almost finished the colony on Mars as an independent entity, and although things were returning to some level of normality, the overall political and economic situation was still precarious. So much so that she had been recalled by the Mars Council and pressed back into the service of the state.

Jann had spent most of her time during the Great Storm, as it had become known, holed up with Nills Langthorp on an opulent orbital station owned and operated by the industrialist, Lane Zebos. It began simply as a short sojourn, a vacation of sorts, but as the storm progressed, eventually engulfing the entire planet, the station had turned into a refuge, albeit for a privileged few.

As the months passed, Jann found herself becoming more and more distant from the trials being experienced by the people living on the planet surface below. It was only when she received a long and detailed report from Mia Sorelli on the chaos that had taken place in Syrtis that she began to realize just how detached she had become from the reality on the ground. She vowed to make amends and returned to Jezero City as soon as flights resumed after the Great Storm. The Council then prevailed upon her to help shore up confidence in the current administration as the reconstruction efforts got underway and the citizens of Mars tried, as best they could, to put the past behind them and return to something akin to normality.

But now this new threat had emerged. Two sols ago, a

ship bound for Earth blew up on the launch pad on the outskirts of Jezero City during a routine ignition test. The failure was catastrophic; all that remained was a shredded hunk of metal and a large crater. Fortunately there were no people on board at the time, nor were there any ground crew present, as the test had been performed remotely.

Yet, buried in the wreckage of the ship lay the charred remains of two bodies, so badly burned that the only way to identify them was through a DNA test, and it was the results of this analysis that were proving to be truly seismic.

"You're saying they're an exact match?" Jann looked over at Dendryte.

"Insofar as a DNA fingerprint can tell. Yes, identical in every way."

"Twins?" Jann offered.

"Possibly." Dendryte pushed his old-fashioned glasses back up his nose. "But twins of this age are rare here on Mars. There are only two pairs in the population, and all four are alive and kicking. So if what we're looking at are indeed twins, then they're not from around here. And, there's no record of twins arriving on the planet since well before the Great Storm."

He paused for a beat and readjusted his glasses again. "The other interesting observation, and the primary reason I brought it to your attention, is that the DNA shows a remarkable similarity to...eh, Xenon Hybrid. I've identified several micro-islands of sequences that are only seen in his DNA."

Jann shifted her gaze back to the lab data. "Yes, I noticed that. I know that signature so well it was the first thing that jumped out at me. Yet"—she paused for a beat —"it's not specifically his, is it?"

"Correct. There are subtle differences. But still, it's very odd."

Jann studied the patterns on the screen again and tried to think about what all of this meant. Xenon Hybrid had an exotic profile, a result of him being an amalgam of several strands of enhanced human DNA. He was unique, and one of the few still alive from that dark period of the colony's past when human cloning and genetic experimentation were practiced without restriction. Some said his DNA was so different that he represented a new human species—less Homo sapien and more Homo ares.

He was also a highly revered individual, and still— technically, at least—the head-of-state. But seeing as how this was a ceremonial post with no power, it allowed room for Xenon's more obvious eccentric behavior. Not many had seen or heard from him for many years. He had removed himself from society and gone wandering, trying to discover the essence of the planet. Gone native, as many would say. Mostly this was seen as a cultural project, and no one minded too much. Many even applauded this walkabout and viewed it as the foundation of a deeper Martian cultural understanding.

Then, around three Earth years ago, he stopped his wandering and established a quasi-spiritual retreat in an old research outpost some fifteen hundred kilometers north of Jezero Crater, deep within a region know as the Plains of Utopia. Since that time, there had been a constant trail of devotees making their way north. And soon, his enclave grew into a community estimated to be around a hundred or so people. No one bothered them, and they bothered no one.

"WHO ELSE KNOWS ABOUT THIS?" Jann said, looking directly at Dendryte.

He screwed his mouth up and shook his head. "No one else, not yet. I almost don't believe what I'm seeing. So I thought it best to, eh...get a second opinion."

Jann nodded. "Good, a wise decision. We need to keep this under wraps for the moment."

He shifted from one foot to the other. "I don't know how long I can keep a lid on things. We're talking about an ongoing investigation, and this is a critical piece of evidence. They'll be expecting the results soon."

Jann considered this for a moment. Dendryte was right: he could only stall for so long before he would have to reveal his analysis. Of course, there was always the possibility that nobody would believe it—she was having a very hard time believing it herself.

"You didn't just bring this to me for a second opinion, Lewis. You know just as well as I do that this raises more questions than it answers. I assume there is no match in the population database for this DNA sample?"

Dendryte nodded, a little sheepishly.

"I think we have to assume these two individuals are clones." Jann gestured back at the screen. "Clones that have been derived, in part, from the DNA of Xenon Hybrid?" Jann said this more as a question than a statement of fact.

"That would be one hypothesis."

"Is there another?"

Dendryte stared at the data for a moment, then slowly shook his head. "None that I would regard as plausible. Yet, who would even have the technological know-how to do this?"

"Who indeed. But it also begs another question. That is, was the destruction of that ship really an accident? And if not, then who's behind all this?"

Dendryte remained silent. He simply stared at the screen as if this simple act would somehow give him the answers.

Jann finally gave a dismissive gesture. "Look, this is all just speculation, nothing more. But I'm saying it to underline the danger of jumping to conclusions. One thing is for sure: there is more to this than meets the eye. That's why we need to keep a lid on it for a few sols while I do some digging and try to find out what the heck is going on."

"I understand." Dendryte nodded. "But I can only sit on this for a few sols at most. If it goes past that, then questions will be asked, or they could simply get someone else to do the analysis and the truth will eventually come out."

"I appreciate that, Lewis. But we might know a lot more in a few sols. Just keep it between us for the moment."

Dendryte nodded again, more emphatically this time. "Okay, I'll do what I can." He turned and walked out, leaving Jann with her thoughts.

She switched on the holo-table and brought up a 3D map of Mars, then zoomed in on the location of Xenon's enclave up in the northern lowlands, in the Plains of Utopia. It was a sizable facility now, far greater than the humble research station it had once been. She stood back as the holo-table slowly rotated the 3D rendering. "What have you been doing up there, Xenon?" she whispered to herself. "Maybe it's time I paid you a visit."

2

NILLS

Nills Langthorp stood in the main hall of the Jezero City Science Museum, folded his arms, and considered the forlorn exhibit that was the final resting place of the droid, Gizmo.

Since all flights out of Jezero were suspended in the wake of the catastrophic accident at the main spaceport, he was now stuck here for longer than planned. So, with time on his hands, he decided to go see his old robotic friend and pay his respects, so to speak.

Even though Gizmo had gone its own way, first attaching itself to Dr. Jann Malbec and later to Mia Sorelli, Nills had always been concerned for it, like how a parent would for their own child. Yet, like a parent, over time he had learned to let go and stop worrying about the little robot. Now though, looking at the droid in this sorry state, he could not help but feel a pang of guilt for not being there when its fate was being decided by the Mars Council.

He stepped over the low, braided rope cordoning off the exhibit, much to the surprise of a few other visitors who had also chosen to kill some time exploring the technical history of the Martian colony.

Nills turned to them and gestured at the exhibit. "Maintenance," he said, then stepped up onto the low plinth.

"Trash would be more like it for that old thing," a young, elegantly dressed man with a distinct Earther look snapped back with a laugh.

Nills ignored him. Instead, he began giving the droid a closer examination. "What have they done to you, Gizmo?" he said to himself, shaking his head. "You look like complete crap."

He ran a hand over the gaping hole in Gizmo's breastplate where it had taken a direct hit from a high-powered plasma weapon. "That's not good."

He bent down, peered in, and started probing with his fingers, feeling out the extent of the damage. After a moment, he extracted his hand, stepped back, and scratched his chin before taking another walk around the machine. He made a slow circuit and arrived back at the start, facing the forlorn robot.

Nills shook his head. "Well, Gizmo, you're all banged up, that's for sure. I'm surprised they didn't just send you to the crusher."

For a long time, he just stood looking at the droid as

memories of past exploits rippled through his mind. *I can't just leave it here to simply be scoffed at by moronic tourists...can I?* He considered this for a while, running through the ramifications, both technical and political, of trying to reanimate the droid. Taking possession of it again would need Council approval, and that would take time—a lot of time, with no guarantee that his request would be successful. In fact, it would be highly unlikely. And even if he did manage it, then there was the considerable technical challenge of rebuilding it. Maybe the droid could be made to work again, but how would he restore its mind? Would it still be the same Gizmo?

His comms pinged. It was a message from Jann. The Council session was over, and she was now free to meet up. Nills took one more look at the droid. "I'm not making any promises, old buddy. You're banged up pretty bad, and parts are still in short supply. Then there's the Council to consider, and you know what they're like."

He turned to go, hesitated, then placed a hand on its shoulder joint. "Hang in there, I'll think of something."

IT NEVER CEASED to amaze Nills how a biologist such as Jann could be so engrossed in politics. For him, it seemed like hell. All that arguing, and backstabbing, and manipulating, just to get something done—crazy. It was so much easier dealing with technical systems, where most problems could be fixed by simply following a logical process. There was nothing logical about politics. Still, Jann seemed happier now that they had returned to Jezero and became more involved with the Council.

They agreed to meet in the great biodome, the oldest sector in Jezero, a place with many memories for both of them. He found her sitting on a low bench beside a small pond, surrounded by lush vegetation and exotic trees. It was quiet, and no one else was around.

Nills nodded a greeting as he caught her eye. "Any word on when flights will resume?"

"Is that all you're worried about?" She said this more as a statement.

"Aren't you?" He sat down beside her.

"Right at this moment, Nills, that's actually the least of my concerns."

"What? Something crop up at the Council meeting?"

"Not exactly." Jann glanced around her as if to check they were alone. "I'm going to tell you something, Nills. But you must promise me that it stays between us." Her voice was low, almost conspiratorial.

"Don't tell me the explosion at the spaceport was sabotage?"

Jann cocked an eyebrow at him. "What makes you think that?"

"It was a joke." He paused, examining her face. "Holy crap, really?"

Jann gave a dismissive gesture. "It has not been ruled in or out at the moment."

"That's a classic politician's answer," Nills replied with a grin.

Jann gave a light laugh. "Yeah, I suppose it is." Then her face turned serious, and she lowered her voice. "There were two bodies found at the scene."

Nills raised an eyebrow.

"So badly burned," she continued, "that we had to identify them using DNA samples. A half hour ago, I obtained the results of that analysis...and you're not going to believe this, but it looks like they're clones. Not only that, their DNA is remarkably similar to...Xenon Hybrid."

Nills wasn't sure if he had heard her correctly. "Clones?"

Jann nodded.

Nills remained silent for a beat. "Is it possible there's an error in the analysis?"

"No error. No mistake."

"I can't believe it. Xenon?"

"I've kept this quiet for the moment. You, me, and Dr. Dendryte, the Head of Forensics, are the only ones who know. But that's only for a few sols. Then it will come out."

Nills shook his head in disbelief. "Xenon was always a bit of an eccentric weirdo, but I just can't see him involved in...cloning, after all he went through."

"Neither can I. That's why I think we should pay a visit to his enclave, up in the Plains of Utopia."

Nills' head snapped around and gave her an

incredulous look. "Are you serious? That's a hell of a journey, and there's no flights, remember?"

"No one knows what's been going on up in that place, Nills. They're very secretive, they even have a vetting process before anyone can visit. But I don't think Xenon would refuse an unannounced visit from you and me, now would he?"

Nills remained silent as he considered this.

"Something very weird is going on." Jann sounded more concerned now. "A ship is destroyed and two bodies show up with identical DNA, and it all seems to lead to Xenon."

Nills shook his head again. "I still can't believe he's involved in something like this. Granted, he's very strange, but he's fundamentally benign. I can't see him doing anything that would undermine the functioning of the colony."

"So, how do you explain the DNA results?"

"Maybe it's a mistake, a contaminated sample. Maybe this guy, what's his name…Dendryte, is setting something up, leading you on a merry dance."

Jann thought for a moment. "I considered this. That's why I did another test myself to verify the initial results. It was the same. So, I think we can rule out any funny business on Dendryte's end."

"Coincidence, then? Could it be just…one of those things?"

"Now you're clutching at straws, Nills. No, whatever is going on has something to do with Xenon, whether we care to admit it or not. If we are going to find answers, then I think we need to pay him a visit."

"Xenon's enclave is what...over a thousand kilometers from Jezero?"

"Yes, and since all flights are grounded, we'll have to do it by rover."

Nills gave a long, slow sigh. "Even if we do this, and I'm not saying I want to, but even if we did, how can you be sure we'll get an audience with the great weirdo himself?"

"Xenon is not going to refuse us after all we've been through together. If he does, then that's a red flag straightaway."

"Can't you just call him up, ask a few questions, save us both a lot of hassle?"

"Yes, I could. But I'd like to do some snooping around that facility to see what's really going on."

"Ahh...so that's the real plan. See if there are any bio-labs, that sort of thing?"

"That's exactly what I mean."

Nills paused again and scratched his chin. "Normally I would say you're letting your paranoia run away with you. But, let's face it, you've got a nose for trouble, and it has been pretty accurate to date."

"So, we go?"

Nills stood up and ran a hand through his hair. "I can't believe I'm getting talked into this." He screwed his mouth up and finally nodded. "Okay. But I really don't think we're going to find anything up there except a bunch of people acting like they live in a nineteenth-century monastery."

"I imagine that's exactly what we'll find, on the surface. But what's going on underneath is what we need to discover."

Nills sat down again and wondered if now would be a good time to mention the droid. "Eh...there is something you could do for me, Jann."

"Sure, what is it?"

"I was thinking. How would the Council feel if I were to reactivate Gizmo?"

Jann's face morphed into borderline incredulity. "Gizmo? You're not serious?"

"Why not? I built it. Technically, it's my droid."

Jann sat back in the seat and looked straight ahead as she thought. "Tricky. It's not so much the droid, per se. It's the issue with its integration into the primary colony AI that's the problem."

"But without that, it's not Gizmo?"

Jann shrugged. "I know." She paused. "Look, let me put out a few feelers, test the waters and see if they can be persuaded. It's the best I can do."

"Okay, thanks." Nills nodded. "You know, I just went to visit it, and, well, I sort of felt that we just abandoned the little guy."

"I understand, I feel that way too sometimes. But it's still just a robot, Nills. You've got to remember that." She grabbed his hand and held it tight. "If it means that much to you, I promise I'll do my best. Okay?"

Nills gave a smile. "Sure, thanks."

They sat in silence for a while just listening to the cascading water from the fountain.

"How long do you think it will take?"

"To fix Gizmo?"

"No, to get to Xenon's enclave."

"Oh, two sols. We could overnight at the Brandon waystation."

"We need to keep this very quiet, not a word to anyone. That means traveling incognito."

"That would mean finding some transport that has had its beacon deactivated." He gave Jann a look. "And that's illegal."

"I think it would be best not to advertise our arrival."

"Gonna take a while to dig up a rover like that. Can't use one of mine."

"How long?"

"A sol or two, maybe sooner."

"Okay, but time is not on our side. I've got Dendryte nailed down for a while, but eventually word will get out, and when it does, that enclave will shut up tighter than an airlock in deep space. So, we gotta move fast."

Nills stood up. "I'd better get to it, then." He leaned down and kissed Jann on the forehead. "And don't worry about Gizmo. I've got a better idea."

"What's that?"

Nills winked. "You'll see." Then turned and headed out of the biodome.

3

MIA

Mia Sorelli had been just an hour away from boarding a ship bound for Earth when the whole goddamn thing blew up on the pad —boom, giant fireball. The Jezero City spaceport now resembled a war zone, with several tons of scrap metal scattered all over the launch pad, which the authorities informed her would take weeks to get operational again. While she was extremely relieved that she had dodged that particular bullet, and happy to still be walking around, she was now stuck on Mars for who knew how long while the clean-up operation got underway.

Worse still, since she had been leaving the planet for good to take up a position as Mars envoy on Earth, everything she owned had already been packed up and stowed away on the ship before it was vaporized into nonexistence. The only things she now possessed were the clothes on her back and the contents of a small travel bag.

After the initial shock of her narrow escape from destiny and the complete loss of her possessions had subsided, she had considered departing from one of the several other spaceports on Mars—possibly Syrtis or even Elysium. But before she could make the necessary arrangements, the Council decided, in the interest of public safety, to ground all flights until a full investigation was carried out. Mia was more than pissed. She now found herself without a place to hole up and wait it out, since she had relinquished the tenancy to her accommodation module that very morning.

But there were upsides to being an envoy in the employ of the Martian state—she was now their responsibility. So, they put her up in one of the many hotels that had begun opening up after the Great Storm —and gave her the royal treatment. The suite was at least four times the size of her own modest accommodation module.

But the hotel was practically empty and mostly run by service droids. A few tourists had begun to trickle back in from Earth, but they were thin on the ground and probably now beginning to regret coming to Mars, because it looked like they might be stuck here for a while. So, after her first night, Mia began cracking up.

She needed to get out and meet some humans, preferably ones that could give her some information on when flights might resume. Fortunately, Bret Stanton, from the Mars Law and Order Department (MLOD), contacted her to arrange a meet. He was rather vague and even evasive with his answers to Mia's barrage of questions, simply saying it was best to talk in person.

They arranged to hook up at the hotel cafe, one of the few that had managed to reopen after the storm—many had not, and probably never would. It was situated along the front of the structure, facing onto what was once a busy plaza back when Jezero had tourists. Now it was like a town out of season, with just a few lost souls wandering aimlessly around.

Mia sat at an outside table, people-watching as she waited. Overhead, a bright sun shone through the vast domed roof, and for a brief moment Mia felt herself almost relax. It was a strange feeling. She realized she didn't care that much about losing all her stuff when the ship blew up. It was almost liberating, and imbued in her a feeling of being untethered, being free. She felt a little giddy and tried to snap out of it. It was probably just shock.

Stanton arrived on foot, accompanied by a young MLOD agent and a beefy looking security droid. He sauntered up to Mia's table and sat down as they exchanged greetings. The young agent and the droid stood off to one side with their backs to them, scanning the plaza.

"Mia." Stanton gave her a big smile, then glanced at the hotel facade. "How you holding up, now that you're slumming it in the Ritz?"

"Just peachy, Bret. Me and the service droids are having a blast." She gestured in the direction of the agent and the security droid. "What's with the backup? Something going on I should know about?"

Stanton's reply was interrupted by the waiter arriving, and by the expression on his face, he was clearly delighted to have some customers.

"Just a coffee," Stanton said with an almost apologetic gesture, as if he was sorry it could not be more.

"Same," said Mia.

The waiter nodded and left.

"So, Bret, when am I getting off this planet?"

Stanton considered this question for a moment, clearly thinking about how best to formulate his reply. "There's been a development."

Mia sighed and sat back in her seat. "A development?" She gave Stanton a hard look. "So, what you're saying is not for a while?"

Stanton glanced around to see where the waiter was, presumably to check if he was out of earshot. He was inside, behind the counter operating the coffee machine. Stanton leaned in a little. "Our initial investigation into the explosion is looking like it might be...more than a simple accident."

Mia hesitated for a moment as she slowly raised her eyebrows at Stanton. "You're saying it was deliberate?"

"I'm saying it's a possibility. Something we're looking into."

Mia gave a long sigh. "What the hell is wrong with this planet? We never seem to catch a break, do we?"

"Sure seems that way."

She sighed again, longer this time, almost visibly deflating. "So what makes you suspect...foul play?"

"Spaceships don't blow up like that." Stanton sat back and waved a hand like he was lazily swatting a fly. "Not like way back in the old days when they were full to the brim with volatile rocket fuel. Interplanetary ships use plasma engines, dramatically safer. Except, this was a plasma-containment failure—a very rare occurrence, almost unheard of." He leaned in a little more and lowered his voice. "And we found something in the wreckage."

He sat back, looked at Mia, and raised a finger at her. "But that's all I can divulge...except for this. They've put me on this investigation. I suppose you could call it a promotion."

"Well, well, Bret. My seat in the department is barely cold and here you are, trying it out for size?"

Bret smiled and gestured again at the hotel. "I don't think you're going to miss it? I mean, Mars envoy and all that."

They sat in silence for a moment before Mia eventually asked the million-dollar question. "Any ideas why anyone would do this?"

"Some. One theory is that the explosion was intended to take place midflight, with a full complement of passengers, leaving no evidence."

Mia shook her head in disbelief. "I could have been on that flight."

"Yes, you could." Stanton paused as his coffee arrived, and hung back on saying more until the waiter was again out of earshot. He took a sip and continued. "There is also the possibility that it could even have been an assassination attempt."

"On who?"

Stanton gave her a slightly inquisitive look, as if to say, *You don't get it, do you?* "You, Mia. You are a Mars envoy now, and the highest-ranking state official on that ship."

"You're not seriously suggesting..." Mia gave a quick glance around, then leaned in and lowered her voice. "You seriously think someone is out to get me?"

"At this point in the investigation, we have to consider everything. It could be the reason for the explosion. Then again, it could be something completely different, or maybe a different target. Nevertheless"—he gestured over at the young MLOD agent—"we've given you some security, just in case."

Mia slumped back in her seat and glanced over at the agent. Judging from his body language, he was doing his best to look tough and in control. Yet it lacked conviction. It was just a facade. Mia reckoned he would be worse than useless if shit hit the fan. She might end up having to look after him. The security droid, on the other hand, could be very handy in a tight spot. "So, you have me babysitting now?"

"Agent Steffen is a solid guy, very trustworthy."

"He may be trustworthy, but is he any good in a fight? He looks to me like he's ready to wet his pants."

"Be nice, Mia." Bret waved a finger at her. "If it comes to it, you won't find him wanting."

Mia replied by way of a resigned scowl. "Let's hope it doesn't come to that." She took a sip of her now cold coffee. "So tell me, seriously, when are flights going to resume?"

Stanton screwed his face up. "Who knows. At the moment, everyone is paranoid there might be another... incident. Therefore we need to beef up checks and inspections. Best guess, two to three weeks"—he wriggled a hand—"give or take."

"So I'm here stuck with Frodo and the droid." She sighed. "Where's he sleeping?"

"I suggest the sofa in your palatial suite."

"Do I have to tuck him in, read him a bedtime story?"

"Hey, like I said, be nice. Anyway, you were complaining you only had droids to talk to. And, eh...the droid's not staying. It's coming back with me."

They sat in silence for a moment as Mia glared at him while digesting the prospect of the next few weeks here on Mars. "Any thought on who might be behind this? Maybe some of our old friends from Syrtis?" Mia finally said, once she had resigned herself to her fate.

"Who knows. Maybe it's just some crazy, or a vendetta, or some ideological nutjob."

"Like those Xenonists? You know, the ones who've been spraying the walls with warnings and prophecies?"

Stanton let out a laugh. "Those guys? The followers of our great cultural icon Xenon? Don't make me laugh, Mia. They're just into love and peace and a return to nature. I can't see any reason why a bunch of pacifists would do something like that. Anyway, gotta go. Stay safe." He jerked his head in the direction of the young MLOD agent. "And be nice." He gave her a quick salute and headed off across the plaza.

4

GIZMO

Nills' desire to reanimate the old droid was not based simply on his emotional response after seeing it in such a sad state in the museum. It was also based on the reality that he had the wherewithal to do it. Having, over the years, established a substantial engineering works on Mars, he not only had the facilities and staff, but more importantly he had the spare parts, which were still in general short supply because new deliveries from Earth had not yet picked up to pre-storm levels.

So, he had the desire, he had the ability, he even had the parts, but what he didn't have was the authority. Yet that was not something Nills generally worried about. If he were to seek permission from the Council it would probably take forever, and might well descend into politics and petty squabbling. No, he had a better idea, and that was shoot first and deal with the fallout later.

In reality, what could they do if he just went ahead and reactivated the droid? Nothing. Sure, they would hop up and down, cite the rules, make a lot of noise, but they couldn't really stop him. Nills knew that, and in the end it seemed the simplest solution all around. Of course, it helped greatly that his company had a maintenance contract with the museum.

So, after meeting with Jann, and confirming his own suspicions on how the Council would react to his request, he swung by his workshop in Jezero and picked up a security tag and a large wheeled tool trolley. He then made his way back to the museum, this time in through the maintenance area.

He presented the security tag to the reader, and the large industrial door rose up. He nodded to the security guard, who nodded back. A few moments later, on his return, he repeated this same action, nodding to the guard. But this time he had the droid secured on the trolley with a tarp covering it. The guard nodded back, and Nills casually strolled out.

LESS THAN TWO hours after his visit to the museum, Gizmo was laid out on a workbench in one of Nills' engineering works on the outskirts of Jezero City. Four engineers gathered around the bench, scratching their heads and wondering if their boss had finally lost his marbles.

"You can't be serious, boss. This thing is ancient."

"Yeah, it's a heap of junk. There's a hole in it the size of an airlock."

"Looks like this guy was on the wrong end of an argument with a plasma blast."

"Why you bothering with this hunk of metal, anyway? We've got plenty of better service droids."

Nills placed a hand on the droid's shoulder joint and looked around at his skeptical crew. "This is no ordinary service droid. This is none other than Gizmo, the very first one I created. And most of you are only here due to its actions in the past."

"So, this is the infamous Gizmo," said Ajay, his lead engineer.

The mood began to shift now that the crew understood the pedigree of the machine they had been tasked to get operational.

"What makes this little guy so special," Nills continued, "is that it has a direct interface to the main colony AI, something no other droid has. With that amount of processing power at its disposal, it's almost sentient."

The crew were now silently eying up the droid with a renewed sense of awe.

"But that's not allowed any more, boss. Even if we get it going, and that's a big if, there's no way we could reconnect to the primary AI."

"Yeah, I know, it's a challenge." Nills nodded.

"It's a bit more than a challenge, boss. It's a non-runner."

Nills knew very well that no matter how good a job his team did in restoring Gizmo, if he could not reconnect to the AI, then Gizmo would, at best, be no better than a basic service droid. Most, if not all, of its primary mind existed with the data-stack of the colony's AI. If he could reconnect, then he had a chance of restoring the droid to its former self. Repairing the physical engineering was the easy part; finding a way to circumvent the tight security protocols surrounding the primary AI was the real challenge.

"Let's cross that bridge when we come to it," he said. "In the meantime, I want this little guy brought back to life."

The crew began migrating closer to the workbench, leaning over and inspecting the machine with a renewed and slightly less skeptical interest. They poked and prodded and began to scrutinize the extent of the damage and assess the task ahead of them.

"A lot of these components are very outdated," said Ajay. "Do you want a full upgrade? I mean it would be quicker, and better. We could just replace parts with newer stuff."

Nills thought about this for a moment. On the one hand, he wanted the old Gizmo back with all its quirky ways. But a lot of that was to do with its personality and less about its physical appearance. And Ajay was right: replacing the outdated with the latest hardware would be infinitely quicker than trying to coax a new life out of the old.

"Do it," he finally said with an emphatic flourish of his hand, then pointed at the droid. "Upgrade everything you can. We may as well, seeing as we have the parts on hand."

"Sure thing, boss," Ajay said as he dragged over a tool trolley.

"Okay, guys, you heard the boss. Let's get to work and bring this bucket of bolts back to life."

NILLS SAT across the desk from Oto DeGroot, chief data analyst for Jezero City's primary AI network. He was a heavyset man in his early forties, with an academically detached demeanor, like he had grander things to ponder and social interaction seemed to get in the way of that.

"No way, Nills. You know I'm happy to help you with anything, but this is asking too much."

"I can't see what the big deal is. The Council was happy to reanimate Gizmo a few months ago, so what's changed?"

"Well, you need to go to them to get the okay. Surely someone in your position would have no problem with that."

Nills waved a hand. "I can't be bothered with all the politics and bureaucracy. I would just be giving some self-important moron an opportunity to make political hay."

"The same goes for me, Nills. If they find out I

facilitated this, then there are certain people who could make my life very difficult."

"But there's no need for anyone to find out, Oto. I just need enough time to make the interface connection and download Gizmo's data-stack." Nills continued with his appeal.

Oto leaned back in his seat and became silent for a moment, giving Nills' request further consideration. "The thing I don't get, Nills, is why you want to do this in the first place. I mean, what's the big deal with this droid?"

"We go back a long way, me and that droid. It's a part of me. I suppose you could say it's a friend. So I can't bear to see it simply...discarded. I feel that I owe it."

"It's just a droid."

"A lot of people have said that, Oto."

"And another thing." He sat forward again. "How are you going to pass this off? I mean, they'll know you've reactivated it and accessed the primary AI. How can you hide that?"

"Sure, they'll know I put it back together, but they won't know how. Anyway, we both know that they can't really stop me if I pull rank on them."

"Yeah, I suppose you're fortunate that you're not just anyone. But interfacing it with the AI, how are you going to explain the droid's cognitive abilities?"

"Who's to say it wasn't all still intact? The damage wasn't as bad as it looked, and its neural-net and data-stack were still viable."

Oto screwed his mouth up. "Hmmm...maybe you

could get away with it"—he waved a hand in the air—"and maybe not. It's still too risky for me. I wish I could help, but you're asking me to put my ass on the line here."

Nills took a moment to marshal his thoughts. True, he was asking a lot from the data analyst, but there really was little or no risk of being found out if they played it smart. Maybe Oto just needed some enticement, something to sweeten the deal. "Say, how's that rover project you're working on going?"

Oto had acquired himself a beaten-up old transport rover a while back, just after the storm settled. It was a non-runner, but serviceable—and with few spare parts around, he got it cheap. But there was a world of work to do to get it running again, even if he could find the parts.

He let out an exasperated sigh. "Don't talk to me about that. It's still sitting in a lockup, costing me money, and parts prices are just crazy at the moment. Not one of my better ideas."

Nills leaned in, placing his elbows on the edge of the desk. "Maybe I could help with that?"

Oto raised his eyebrows. "Ahhh, no. I see where you're going with this, trading me some spare parts. I'll admit it's tempting, but no."

"I wasn't talking about spare parts. I was thinking of rebuilding it for you."

The analyst gave him a curious look, as if he wasn't sure what he was hearing.

"What's the power source? Methane?" Nills asked.

"Yeah, old school."

"Could swap it out for a compact fusion reactor, virtually unlimited range. Give it to me now and I can put a team on it, bring it back in a few sols. Could be very handy to have working, now that all flights are grounded."

"Fusion power source, did you say?"

"Drives smooth as glass, and a two-million-kilometer range."

Oto shook his head and slumped back in his seat again. "Goddammit, Nills, you must really like that droid. Okay, you got me. What do you need?"

"Thanks, Oto. I really appreciate this."

He waved a dismissive hand, "Yeah, yeah, just don't make me regret this, Nills."

5

ALL WIRED UP

Jann walked quietly through the access tunnel, heading for the old industrial sector of Jezero City. It was an area that had undergone a long, slow decline, starting way before the Great Storm.

When the city became the administrative capital of Mars and a primary tourist hub, the heavy industry that had populated this sector started moving out, some to the northern part of the Jezero Crater, some over to Syrtis in the east or even Elysium in the west. But a few still remained. Light industry mostly, those that serviced the needs of a population based on administration, wealthy inhabitants, and tourism. Yet many of those had still struggled during the Great Storm.

As she moved through the sector, she passed numerous shuttered and dilapidated units, all signs of the toll that period had on the viability of these industries to survive. It was a sad sight, and one that had little hope of recovery, particularly if the recent incident at the spaceport was not resolved satisfactorily.

But the health of the Martian economy was not what concerned Jann. No, it was the possibility of a return to a dark past. In her mind, there was only one possible explanation for the identical DNA of the bodies they had found—they were clones. And if that turned out to be true, then there was something far more sinister going on than just the threat of moribund economic activity.

Overhead lights flicked on as she moved, illuminating the way forward. She pulled on the hood of her cloak so as to obscure her face from any cameras that might still be operating in this sector. Underneath the cloak she wore a light EVA suit, suitable for short excursions on the planet surface, the helmet and gloves stowed in a backpack. It was probably overkill; they shouldn't need to go full EVA. But this was Mars, where it paid to be prepared.

She eventually entered into a wide, open area that provided access to the larger industrial units. She was now at the very extremity of the eastern side of the city.

Jann found the door she was looking for. Above it, in large faded letters, was a simple sign reading Langthorp Tech. She presented her eye to the retinal scanner and the door clicked open into a dimly lit, domed expanse. Here and there, drifting out of the shadows, she could see the shapes of several rovers and utility vehicles in varying states of repair. A multitude of dismembered droids also looked out from the shadows, like a theater of ghosts. A low background hum provided the soundtrack. It all felt a little eerie.

Most of the light illuminating the workshop area spilled out through a long, windowed side area. Behind it, she could see Nills standing with his back to her, looking intently at a bank of monitors that seemed to be scrolling through thousands of lines of code. As she approached, she could see a droid all wired up to some interface— presumably Nills was working on it.

It was not a standard service droid. It looked like an obsolete model, and it reminded her of Gizmo. Except this one looked more robust. *Poor Gizmo*, she thought. *Just an exhibit now.*

"Nills, shouldn't we be getting ready to go?"

Nills turned around and waved a hand. "I just need to get this done, then we can go. Sorry, but it's the only time I can get to do this."

Jann moved over beside Nills and glanced at the screens. "What are you working on?"

He gestured at the droid. "Recognize it?"

"Looks like Gizmo, but that's parked in the museum."

"Was." He smiled. "I rescued the little guy, and the team here rebuilt it."

"What? You're joking me. We're supposed to be keeping a low profile. There'll be hell to pay for doing that."

Nills waved a hand. "Ah, screw them. What are they going to do?"

Jann sighed and shook her head. She should have known that Nills might pull a stunt like this. "Make life difficult, for one. You seem to forget, Nills, that your actions also reflect on me. I'm back to being a Council member, and this looks bad."

Nills lowered his head a bit. "Sorry, Jann. I...just couldn't leave it to rot in the museum, or go through the torture of trying to get Council approval. Anyway, I'll take the heat."

Jann went silent for a moment. Nills had just pulled a fait accompli, and there was not much she, or anyone else, could do about it now. But before she could remonstrate him any further, the droid twitched, then began to move its limbs very slowly.

"What's it doing?" she asked, taking a step back.

"Self-test. It has new appendages, so it's figuring out its new geometry."

Jann stood for a moment, a little mesmerized by this robotic tai chi. "I thought it was so damaged that it would never operate again."

"Fortunately there was still a backup on its mind in the central AI." He turned and gestured at the screens. "That's what I'm doing now, restoring its cognition."

Jann raised an eyebrow. "You hacked into the primary colony AI?"

"Eh, not exactly. I called in a few favors."

Jann shook her head. "If any of this ever gets out, I'm going to disown you, Nills."

Nills gave a laugh. "Ha, don't worry. Even if it does, it will all blow over eventually."

Gizmo stopped moving, prompting Nills to swing around on his chair and check the screens again. "It's finished." He looked back at the droid expectantly. Nothing happened for a moment—then it spoke.

"Nills Langthorp and Doctor Jann Malbec, what a pleasant surprise. How nice to see you"—it paused for a beat—"after all this time. My last data entry is of a high-energy plasma blast heading my way."

"Gizmo? Is that really you?" Despite Jann's annoyance at Nills' complete disregard for protocol, she now felt a ripple of excitement at the prospect of the robot's resurrection.

"Yes, it is I, Gizmo."

Nills punched the air. "I knew it. I knew I could get you back."

"It would appear I have been sojourning in the museum, yet again."

"Yeah, everyone thought you were a goner last time," Jann said, her excitement audible in her voice. "But Nills thought otherwise."

"Well, I am very grateful. Thank you." It proceeded to examine some of the new upgrades. "And it seems I have become somewhat more robust in the process."

"I thought I might as well bring you up to spec," said Nills.

The robot began to move around, leaving the area they were in and heading out onto the workshop floor, where it zoomed back and forth, testing out its newfound abilities.

"Are we taking it with us?" Jann asked.

"I reckon so. Could be useful. Let's face it: it's saved our asses before, so it would be almost reckless not to bring it."

"I suppose. Anyway, it's getting late. We need to go soon."

Nills flicked off the screens, picked up a backpack he had lying on a seat, and headed out to the workshop area. "Come on then, this way." He stopped beside a beaten-up old six-wheeled rover, activated the outer door, and clambered in.

Jann followed, a little skeptical, then Gizmo. "Are you sure this will get us there and back? It looks like it's seen better days. Can't we use one of your fleet rovers?"

Nills began powering up the rover's systems. "The problem is that they're classified as official vehicles, so they all have tracking beacons. Central would know exactly where we are, and even who's on board."

"Ah, I see. So, we're stuck with this." She rubbed a finger along the back of a dusty seat.

"Sorry, Princess—you'll have to get your hands dirty. But this machine is completely off-grid. My crew here have retrofitted a new power system and given it a thorough overhaul. It actually belongs to a client, but we can put it down to a road test." He sat down in the pilot seat. "Gizmo? I need you up here."

The droid moved up into the cockpit.

"Think you can navigate this machine to the Brandon waystation?"

"My pleasure," Gizmo said as it moved into the cockpit and interfaced with the rover's systems.

Jann strapped herself into a seat next to Nills. The outer door closed, sealing them in, and the machine began to move into the main facility airlock. Once the pressure was equalized, the outer door opened and they moved out across the surface of Jezero Crater, heading northwest and ultimately into the Plains of Utopia.

6

OUR SOL WILL FALL

Mia watched Stanton and the security droid disappear around a far corner of the plaza, leaving her to her thoughts and her new bodyguard—who was standing alert a short distance away, still doing his best to look confident in his new role. *Great*, she thought. *Stuck here for who knows how long, babysitting a rookie.* She sighed, flagged the waiter, and ordered another coffee—not much else to do.

While she waited, her mind turned to who might want to kill her. Sure, there were a few people that might hold a grudge or two. She had stepped on quite a few scumbags and lowlifes over the past few years as an agent with the MLOD. But was there anyone that really hated her to the extent that they would try to kill everyone on a ship just to get rid of her?

None came to mind. And she was certain that no one on the quick mental list she had compiled had the technical skill to implement such a bold plan. Could she really have been a target?

The more she thought about it, the more she reckoned that Stanton, and others in the department, were just covering their asses. They were simply looking at all possible motivations, and so it would be prudent not to rule out the possibility. Yet, she could sense from the rookie they'd sent her that they weren't really convinced she was a target. So if it wasn't her, then who? Or was it something else entirely? Or was it just a technical failure?

She glanced over at the young ag... "Hey, what's your name again?"

"Zack Steffen, ma'am."

"Just call me Mia."

"Yes, ma...eh, Mia."

"Come over here and sit down. You're making me nervous hovering around like that."

Zack looked a little unsure if he should comply with this request. Mia reckoned he was probably searching through the official rulebook in his head, trying to find the correct protocol to implement in such a circumstance.

"Hey, Zack, just chill. We're not on a training mission, I'm not scoring you out of ten. We just have to get along for the next few weeks until flight restrictions are lifted. Trust me when I say no one is trying to kill me, okay?"

Zack nervously glanced left and right, as if checking for some unknown threat that was about to pounce at any moment.

"Come on, sit." Mia pointed to the seat in front of her. "Let me get you a coffee." She turned and caught the waiter's eye.

Zack finally relented, sitting down with the actions of someone who'd just had a great weight lifted from his shoulders.

Mia studied him for a beat. He was not as young as she had first thought. He just had one of those boyish faces that some men are cursed with. Cursed in that they're forever doomed to never be taken seriously, until that time when the years finally catch up and they look at themselves in the mirror and realize they've turned into an old man overnight. She almost felt sorry for him.

"And it's obvious that the department doesn't think so, either," Mia continued.

"What makes you think that?" he said, adjusting the position of his plasma pistol to get more comfortable in the seat.

"Because they sent me you, Zack. Let's face it, you're not exactly a one-man killing machine."

Zack raised a hand. "That's a little unfair. I know I don't have a lot of experience in the field, but..."

Mia cut him off. "Trust me, I've met a few killers in my day, and you're not one of them. Faced with the cold, hard reality of a life-and-death situation, you'll probably just shoot yourself. So, here's the deal, Zack. If you and I are to get through the next few weeks, then you do what I say, when I say it—or I can just shoot you now and get it over with."

Zack remained mute for a moment, considering this onslaught on his self-esteem by the very person he was supposed to protect. "Eh, with all due respect..."

Mia raised a hand to stop him. "Sorry, Zack, maybe that was a little harsh of me. Look, I'm sure you're probably top of the class for whatever. But if for some inexplicable reason we get into a *situation,* then it will be me looking after you. No offense."

Zack said nothing for a moment before finally realizing that he was not going to win an argument with Mia Sorelli. "That's okay," he finally said. "In fact, it's kind of a relief. I don't know how long I could have kept up the pretense." Zack slumped down in his seat and relaxed.

Mia gave a laugh. "Ha, I think you and me are going to get along just fine."

They sat for a while in silence, waiting for the waiter to bring the coffee.

"Must be short-staffed here," Zack finally said as he pointed to the wall to one side of Mia. "They haven't cleaned off the graffiti yet."

Mia glanced around a little absent-mindedly, wondering what Zack was on about. Sure enough, the side wall of the cafe was covered in scratches and badly rendered motifs. It seemed that people had been using walls as a canvas ever since humanity had learned how to make a mark, and Jezero City was no exception.

"Normally they clean that stuff off as soon as it appears," Zack continued. Mia considered that he might be planning to hunt down the perpetrators of this heinous crime. "But it looks like they haven't gotten around to it yet."

"Lot of catching up to do. Lot of places just trying to get by at the moment," Mia replied as one particular scrawl caught her eye. It was in bold red paint, signed with a little *X*, like a kiss.

"*Our sol will fall*." She turned back to look at Zack. "I've seen that one around a few places. Any idea what it means?"

The coffee arrived. Zack took a sip. "It means our day will come. It's Xenonist propaganda. You can tell from the *X*."

Mia was tempted to look around again, but resisted. "How come you know that? Are you into all that stuff?"

Zack nearly spat his coffee out. "No way, they're really just a cult."

"I thought they were simply followers of the great Xenon Hybrid?"

Zack's face screwed up in disgust. "Maybe they were at some point. Now they're just a bunch of weirdos with an unhealthy obsession."

"So how come you know so much about them?"

"They have one of their clearing houses right across from where I live. I've been following them for a while."

"Really?" Mia leaned back in her seat and relaxed a little. Zack may be completely useless as a bodyguard, but at least he seemed chatty, and actually quite easygoing. He would make better company over the next few sols than talking to service droids. "So, what goes on in this *clearing house*?" she prompted.

Zack's body language began to soften. Here was an area he had some knowledge of, and he seemed happy to share it with Mia. Clearly he was more of a nerd than a hard-ass. Better suited to investigation and analysis than knocking heads together.

"Anyone who wants to visit Xenon's enclave up north must be vetted first. They have a *clearing house*, here in Jezero. People go in, get checked out, and then are transported up to Xenon's outpost."

"Seems eminently sensible to me. He's still technically the head-of-state. Wouldn't be good for some crazy to try and take a pop at him."

"Yeah, of course, but..." He trailed off. "Ah...I'm sure you're not interested in my theories."

"Theories?" Mia prompted again.

"Doesn't matter." He waved a dismissive hand.

"Don't go all shy on me now, Zack. Just when things were getting interesting. Go on, tell me more. We've got lots of time to kill."

Zack gave her a considered look, clearly wondering how much to say. He gave a quick glance around, then sat forward. "Back during the Great Storm, there was little or no activity at this clearing house. No unnecessary travel and all that. But over the last few months, activity has been increasing, a lot of coming and going. Not unusual in and of itself, yet...there's something going on. Can't quite put my finger on it, it's just some odd activity and weird coincidences."

"Like what?" Mia found herself becoming more intrigued.

He cocked his head. "Weird stuff. Don't know if it means anything, but..." He paused for a beat as he thought. "I have a direct view of the place from my window, so I get to see a lot of the activity. A few weeks ago, I spotted a strange-looking guy leaving and getting into a ground car. No big deal, you might say, but a few minutes later the very same guy came out of the building again, which doesn't make any sense.

"I reckoned it must be an identical twin and thought no more about. Then, a sol or two later, I saw two women leave. Both were identical. Another set of twins? What are the chances of that? As you can imagine, this got me intrigued, so I, eh...kept a closer eye on the people entering and leaving, and I'm now pretty convinced we have a very high incidence of identical twins here in Jezero."

Mia thought about this for a moment. "That is a bit weird, alright."

"The other thing is, a month or so ago I couldn't sleep so I got up and sat in my usual spot beside the window, when I noticed they were taking delivery of a number of large crates. Again, no big deal, but why the middle of the night? Over the course of that week, they had deliveries coming every night. And it looked to me that they were trying to be very quiet about it."

"Interesting," Mia agreed. "What do you think is going on?"

Zack shook his head. "No idea, but it's odd. Strange people, strange deliveries, and all this Xenonist graffiti showing up all at the same time."

"Hmmm...could be the seeds of a good conspiracy theory," Mia offered.

Zack gave a sigh and said nothing.

"Wait a minute..." Mia raised an index finger at him. "You went to the department with this, didn't you?"

Zack stared into his coffee cup.

"And they laughed you out of the place. In fact, they probably gave you me to look after as punishment."

Zack looked up at her a little sheepishly. "Something like that."

Mia gave him a long, considered look. "Maybe you and I should go a take a deeper look at these guys."

Zack's face brightened.

"Maybe, as a Mars envoy, I want to go see Xenon before I leave for Earth. In which case, we should pay this *clearing house* a visit, poke them a bit, do some sneaking around, and see what reaction we get?"

"You mean...actually go in there?" Zack's face brightened even further.

"That's exactly what I mean." Mia wasn't sure, but she thought she heard Zack gulp.

7

THE BRANDON WAYSTATION

Jann woke to a nudge from Nills. "We're almost at the waystation. It's just a few kilometers away." Nills pointed ahead.

She shifted in her seat, sat up, and looked out the rover's windshield. It was pitch black outside, the vast panoply of dazzling stars overhead providing little in the way of illumination, only serving to demarcate the silhouette of the horizon. The lights from the rover punched through the darkness and afforded them a small window on the road ahead.

Soon they began to pick out the halo from the illumination around the waystation. A vague outline of the facility began to materialize. It was sizable, and as they drew closer, Jann could see it was comprised of several domed structures with two long docking bays for rovers, like wings reaching out on either side of the complex. Most of the ports were unoccupied.

"Looks quiet," she said. "Still, we'll need to be careful in there and not give ourselves away. We should try and pass ourselves off as a couple of random travelers."

Nills nodded. "Well, I need to eat some food, I'm starving. We can return to the rover after, and get some rest before pushing on."

Jann glanced around at the rough, utilitarian interior. "Yeah, a little uncomfortable in here, not much in the way of creature comforts. Maybe we could get a module, get some proper rest, and freshen up."

"I thought we're pressed for time?" said Nills.

"Yes, we are. But we still need to be sharp. Better to get some real sleep while we can."

"Okay, but there's always the possibility of running into someone traveling to or from Xenon's enclave. If this enterprise of yours is based on the element of surprise, then we don't want to be recognized, and then for some conscientious follower to tip off the enclave that we're on our way up there."

"Just keep our interaction to an absolute minimum," Jann said, sounding a little tired.

"We have been allocated docking bay B7, just over there," Gizmo interjected, as it pointed out a vacant area along the left-hand docking wing of the facility.

"Okay, Gizmo. Can you take us in, and make sure you don't transfer any data that might identify us once we connect."

"Certainly."

The rover adjusted its speed and direction as the

droid maneuvered it in toward the docking bay. Dust kicked up from the rover's wheels, clouding over the lights illuminating the bay as Gizmo reversed the machine into position. There was a thump followed by a series of alerts flashing up on the cockpit dash.

"Secure connection established, pressure equalized," Gizmo said, detaching its interface and moving out of the cockpit.

Jann was already standing beside the airlock. A scarf covered her mouth and nose, and the hood of her cloak obscured most of her face. Nills followed. "Gizmo, come. You may as well join us."

"Maybe Gizmo should stay here?" said Jann. "It might attract attention."

"I doubt it. You'll see more weirdness in this place than a medieval circus. It'll be fine."

They moved through the airlock and into a dimly lit, deserted corridor, which brought them out into a wide, circular common area. A clump of tables with seating occupied the central area—none of which seemed to match. Some were old industrial units, others repurposed rover and shuttle seating. Around the circumference of this space, vending stations and information portals blinked and flashed for the customers' attention. Several corridors led off to other sectors of the facility. The lighting was subdued, yet Jann could make out a few knots of people and droids, some eating, some resting, others utilizing the vending stations.

They walked over to one with a brightly illuminated

noodle sign, *Djinn Ramen–100% Bio-Engineered*, and after a few moments managed to extract something that approximated food. Jann poked a spork into a steaming bowl of ramen in an attempt to identify its ingredients. They took a seat in a darkened section—as far away from any of the other diners as possible.

"Looks quiet enough," said Nills as he scanned the area. "If we're going to stay the night here, then we will need to book a module with a fake ID. Fortunately, I came prepared." He whipped out an ID chip with the flourish of a magician. "Something I made earlier."

"You know that's illegal," said Jann with a look of mock disapproval.

Nills winked. "I won't tell if you don't. Gizmo?" The droid tilted its head in his direction. "Scan this ID, and use it for one of the booking portals here to get us an accommodation module. Make sure it's on the surface, nothing subterranean...and the best they have. Okay?"

A ruby red ribbon of light flashed from Gizmo's sensor array as the droid read the information from the ID chip. Then it moved off to execute the request.

"Don't look now, but over to your right are two people that may have taken an interest in us," Jann said in between mouthfuls of ramen.

Nills didn't look; he just kept eating. "Oh?"

"They have those dark-red cloaks that the Xenonists sometimes wear."

"Then we should probably hurry up. It's not outside the bounds of possibility that we might be recognized."

Jann had only taken a few more mouthfuls before she sensed a shadow being cast over their table. She looked up to see one of the cloaked figures standing beside them.

"Pardon me for interrupting your food, but my colleague and I were wondering if you are traveling north and might have room for two pilgrims?"

Nills waved a hand. "No, we're, eh...not going north. We're heading for Bauford, over to the west. Now if you don't mind, we're both very tired after many hours of travel."

"My apologies. Sorry for troubling you." The figure took a step back.

"That's okay," Nills said with a nod.

The pilgrim bowed, but instead of leaving, he focused his attention on Jann. "Forgive me, but you look remarkably like Dr. Jann Malbec."

Jann caught a glance from Nills. Had they just been rumbled? She gave a short laugh. "Ha, I get that all the time. But no. Sorry to disappoint."

Nills gave a gesture to suggest to the pilgrim that it was time to get lost.

He bowed again, more formally this time, and moved away.

"Do you think he bought it?" Jann whispered.

"Let's hope so. But it might be best to get out of sight in case anyone else gets nosy." Nills lifted his head and looked around. "Now, where's Gizmo got to?"

"Here," the droid said as it approached their table. "I have obtained an accommodation module as requested."

Then it lowered the amplitude of its voice, almost to a whisper. "I have also secured the IDs of all the other guests at this establishment. For no other reason than because I could." It gestured with one of its appendages.

Nills raised an eyebrow. "Very good. A little over and above the call of duty, Gizmo. But good work nonetheless." He nodded to Jann. "Ready?"

"Yeah, let's get out of here."

They cleared up their food trash, and Gizmo led the way to their room for the night.

JANN COULDN'T SLEEP. She tossed and turned, and after an hour or so she simply gave up trying. So instead, she got up, made herself some tea, and sat by the large viewing window looking out onto the nighttime landscape. She flicked through the guest list that Gizmo had downloaded onto her slate, trying to find the guy who had recognized her earlier.

She didn't get a good look at him, so it wasn't so easy, but after eliminating all guests that were clearly not pilgrims, she had narrowed it down to just a handful. Yet, there was one face that looked vaguely familiar to her, even if the name didn't ring any bells—John Richards. Somewhere in the back of her mind, she thought she had met this person before, but where and in what context, she couldn't remember.

She sighed, took a sip of tea, and put the slate away. Maybe she was just being paranoid. There was no reason to think he really did twig who she was. And even if he did, so what. He would probably think nothing of it, considering that Nills had let it be known they were heading for the Bauford Research Station. She was just a little rattled by it, nothing more. Jann finished her tea, gave a sigh, and satisfied herself that it was absolutely nothing to worry about.

8

THE ORDER OF XENON

Kim Han-su, prioress of the Order of Xenon in Jezero City, stood before a large wall monitor in her otherwise spartan quarters and studied a series of grainy images that cascaded across the display. They showed two people and their droid partaking in a hasty meal in the Brandon waystation some eight hundred kilometers north of Jezero. But as she studied the images, the key question in Han-su's mind was whether the woman in the image was, or was not, Dr. Jann Malbec.

It had been brought to her attention by an acolyte en route to the Order's primary enclave farther north, in the Plains of Utopia. Sometime in the past, this particular acolyte had been an associate of Malbec's, and as such recognized her. But it had been at least a decade since he had any interaction with her, so he couldn't be one-hundred percent sure. However, when he approached her, the woman claimed that she was not Malbec. Which could be true, but then again, she could be lying—in which case, this only added to the mystery. Was it really her? And if so, what was she was doing there, and why was she traveling incognito?

What convinced the acolyte to forward this information to his superior was the fact that the man traveling with her looked remarkably like Nills Langthorp. Even their droid had similarities to one they had both been known to utilize—one that had been stolen from the science museum very recently. If this was indeed Malbec and Langthorp, then it raised a considerable number of questions in Han-su's mind—along with a rising sense of panic.

Malbec had not been seen in public for quite some time. During the Great Storm, she had taken a backseat in the affairs of the colony. Most thought she had simply gone into retirement, leaving the workings of the colony to others. Yet here she was, in an isolated waystation, traveling with none other than Nills Langthorp. What the hell was she up to?

The waystation in question was at the crossroads of a number of industrial and research facilities that existed around that region of Mars. But most of the traffic utilizing it was either traveling to or from the Order's primary enclave. Was Malbec on her way up there? She and Langthorp were old friends of Xenon's, so it was not outside the bounds of possibility.

Kim Han-su gave a deep sigh and resigned herself to

the unenviable task of passing this information further up the line, and that meant calling Argon Noble, abbot of the enclave and current leader of the entire Order. She reached out and gestured at the screen to initiate the call and transmit the report along with the image files. A few moments later, a 3D holographic avatar of Argon blossomed into life above the holo-table.

"Prioress Han-su, this is concerning news that you send. It seems we now have to contend with the very real possibility of Dr. Jann Malbec and Nills Langthorp paying an unannounced visit to our enclave—no doubt their intention is to meet Xenon Hybrid. This, as you can imagine, is not what we need right now.

"And while I commend you for bringing this to my attention, I might add that it's as a direct consequence of your failed attempt on the Earth-bound spaceship. Malbec knows something and is coming to snoop around —of this I am certain." The avatar flicked and bristled as if it was operating in sympathy with the Abbot's thinly veiled anger.

"My mortification at this failure knows no bounds, Abbot, and I humbly subject myself to your disfavor and those of the brethren." The prioress did her best to not upset Argon Noble any more than she could possibly manage.

"Your desire for redemption is duly noted, Prioress Han-su, and there may well be an opportunity for your martyrdom in the coming sols. But our priority now is to focus on the problem of Malbec and Langthorp."

Han-su's attempts at throwing herself at Argon's mercy were only succeeding in digging a deeper hole. She needed to change tack, start offering solutions, prove her worth to the Order.

"They...eh...could be taken care of," she said, a little hesitantly.

"They will, Prioress. But not in the idiotic manner I think you're suggesting. You need to realize that they are founders of the colony, they go way back to the beginning. In short, Prioress, they are not people who can simply be brushed off. If their intention is to venture north to the enclave, then they will expect Xenon to receive them, and if this does not happen, they could cause us a lot of trouble. So, Prioress, this is exactly what will happen—they will meet Xenon Hybrid."

Han-su's eyes widened. "Is...is that possible?"

"With a certain sleight of hand." The avatar grinned. "Hopefully, it will be enough to satisfy them. However, we now need to move the timeline forward."

"But..." Han-su felt the panic rising within her.

"No buts. This has now become a necessity. We can only stall Malbec for so long. Time is not on our side."

"Of course, we are here to serve." The Prioress thought it best to return to being conciliatory.

"The date for Ares to Arise must now be brought forward by seven sols."

Han-su reckoned this to be an almost impossible task, and just for a brief moment considered pleading with the abbot for more time, but there was no point. She would just have to find a way.

"Of course, a way will be found. We of the Jezero chapter will not fail."

"See to it that you don't, or you will be given the opportunity to become a martyr sooner than you think."

The holographic avatar extinguished, and Han-su could breathe a little easier. *This is my own fault,* she thought. If she had not been so enthusiastic in her desire to impress the upper echelons of the Order by attempting such an audacious attack on the Earth-bound ship, then maybe they would not be in this position now. Yet all was not lost. The serendipitous discovery of Malbec at the waystation gave the enclave an advantage; they knew she was on her way, steps would be taken to contain the risk. Han-su should be rewarded for alerting the enclave, not put under even more pressure.

Her comms unit pinged. *What now?* she thought. She glanced at the screen. It was a call from Admissions, down at the entrance atrium of the House. *What the Ares do they want?* She hit connect.

With that, a video feed materialized on the wall monitor showing a wide-angle shot of the atrium. Two people were engaged in a conversation with a follower at reception.

"Prioress Han-su, we have a situation down here," came a breathy voice.

"This better be important," Han-su replied, with no attempt to disguise her exasperation.

"Eh...it's Mia Sorelli. You know, the Mars envoy. She's in the atrium. She's requesting a visit to the enclave. What should I do?"

"Get rid of her, spin her some story, just don't make her suspicious of anything. Wait a minute...where's that guy going?"

On the camera feed, Han-su could see that Sorelli's associate had disappeared; he was no longer in view. She gestured at the screen to bring up some of the other camera feeds in the House. She found him strolling down one of the private corridors.

"He's gone inside the building," Han-su shouted. "In the main corridor—he's opening doors. He's in the lab." She was becoming frantic. "Get him the hell out of there, now!"

Two followers raced into the lab, confronted the intruder, and escorted him back out to the atrium, where he reconnected with Sorelli. There was a brief exchange of apologies and pleasantries, and then they left.

Han-su breathed a sigh of relief, yet it was only momentary. This was a major breach in security. Sorelli was a well-known ex-cop of some repute, and Han-su knew damn well she was not here to enquire about visiting the enclave. She and her sidekick were poking around, trying to peer into the darker corners of the Order's House here in Jezero, and one of them had seen the lab. They would be back, perhaps not so overtly. And the next time, they might not see them coming. Security would need to be beefed up, but even still, Han-su knew she was dealing with a formidable foe in Mia Sorelli, if her reputation was anything to go by.

The vultures were circling. First Malbec's journey to the enclave, now this. Deep down, the prioress knew she was partly responsible. Had she not sanctioned the attack on the spaceship, none of this would be happening. But she had so desperately desired the adulation of the Order. How else was she to rise through its ranks if not through bold action to advance its objectives? And to some degree, the attack had not been a complete failure. Flights had stopped, no more people arriving, and the wheels of commerce were grinding to a halt. All the better for the Order. All the better for their time to arise.

Yet there were some practical concerns that simply could not be willed out of existence, and more production time was needed. Han-su could not afford another mistake. Sorelli would have to be taken care of. An opportunity for martyrdom, perhaps. Not for Han-su, of course. That privilege would given to some other blessed soul.

9

PLAINS OF UTOPIA

Jann, Nills, and Gizmo spent the night in the waystation without further incident. They slipped away in the morning quietly and unnoticed, disconnecting the rover from its docking bay by overriding the station's security systems, and leaving no digital trace of having ever been there. Gizmo navigated the machine out from the waystation, shifting it northward toward the enclave of Xenon Hybrid while Jann and Nills settled in for the long journey ahead.

After a few hours of traveling, they began to enter into the region known as the Plains of Utopia, a vast, flat expanse of land extending as far as the unbroken horizon ahead. The road was in good repair, as much as any could be on Mars, considering all roads were dirt tracks, even the main transport arteries. Twice they met another rover coming in the opposite direction. It was the most exciting thing that happened on the long, boring journey.

After several hours of this monotony, a faint deviation began to grow out of the horizon, and as they drew closer, Jann began to make out the outline of Xenon's fabled enclave, a population outpost on the very outer limit of colonization on Mars.

A vast domed carbuncle ringed with numerous communications towers grew out from the horizon. Around its base, more structures began to rise up as they advanced. Soon they could see that this was a sizable outpost, as big as a small town, and that was just on the surface. Nills informed her that there was also a significant underground substructure, at least three times the size of what was visible from up top.

The cockpit comms burst into life. "This is Utopia Station One. Six-wheeled rover advancing on southern route, please identify yourself."

Jann glanced over at Nills. "What do you think? Should we comply?"

"I thought that was the plan—surprise them with our arrival."

Jann looked back out through the rover windshield at the looming outline of Xenon's isolated enclave. "Yep, that's the plan. Okay, let's see what happens." She tapped an icon on the comms panel. "This is Dr. Jann Malbec and Nills Langthorp, requesting permission to visit the enclave."

Jann sat back, looking across at Nills as they waited

for a response. It came sooner than either of them thought.

"We welcome you to our community. Please make your way to docking bay A5."

"Well that was a surprisingly fast response," said Jann. "I thought our arrival would throw them into a tailspin."

"Doesn't sound like it. Seems almost routine. Maybe this trip will be more pleasant than we thought," Nills said with a grin. "Actually, I'm looking forward to meeting Xenon again after all this time."

"Maybe," Jann replied, a little unconvincingly.

GIZMO REVERSED the rover into the appointed docking bay, and as soon as a secure connection was confirmed and the cabin pressure equalized with the facility's, both airlock doors were opened. Three figures, all in dark-red cloaks, faced them as they exited. A woman stood out front, her hood down, her face brimming with a bright smile. The two others stood behind her, their hoods up, concealing their faces in shadow.

"We are delighted and overjoyed that you should see fit to grace our humble community with your presence," the woman said, a little ostentatiously. "My name is Anna. I've been assigned to your care during your stay."

Her smile momentarily lost a little of its luster as Gizmo moved out from the rover.

"I'm very sorry, but droids are forbidden in our sanctum. It will not be allowed to enter."

"What? I am not staying here all on my own." Gizmo waved an arm around.

"I'm sorry, Gizmo, but those are the rules," Nills said, the disappointment apparent in his voice. "You'll have to wait for us in the rover."

"Well that is just great. I never get to join in the fun."

"We won't be long," Jann offered. "We'll be back soon."

Gizmo seemed to deflate slightly as it turned around and moved back into the rover. "Left on my own, again." The outer airlock door to the rover closed.

"That's, eh...a very unusual droid you have, or maybe things have moved on a lot since I last encountered one. Anyway, I'm very sorry that you have to do without your mechanical friend, but we have no robots in this sanctum. Everything here is done by our brethren. This is our way." She smiled her best smile.

"That okay," said Jann. "We can manage without it for a while."

"Come, we have prepared some lodgings for you where you can refresh after your long journey." The woman turned on her heel and moved off, beckoning them to follow. The two hooded figures took up the rear.

"When do we get to see our old friend, Xenon?" Jann ventured.

"Master Xenon is meditating at present. But he has been informed of your arrival and is looking forward to meeting you later, after you've had time to rest and recuperate from your journey."

They entered into a large industrial elevator that had seen better sols and descended down a level, where they emptied out into a wide, circular rock cavern. The entire roof seemed to glow with a soft, even illumination. Jann nudged Nills and pointed up at it. "Bioluminescence," she said. "I haven't seen that used in quite a while."

"Me neither, I thought it simply went out of fashion."

"Here we are," said Anna, her smile almost splitting her face in half. A low door set into the wall swung open to reveal a large circular room with a domed roof and the same overhead illumination. The walls were covered with numerous tapestries designed in muted colors and abstract patterns. At the far end was a large, comfortable bed piled high with cushions made in a similar style to the wall hangings. There were benches, tables, and a myriad of rough-hewn sculptures and ornaments dotted around. Red, brown, and yellow were the predominant colors. The entire space had a rustic, almost tribal feel.

"I do hope you find our humble lodgings comfortable," Anna said, a little apologetically. "You'll find a washroom over there, and we have left you some food and refreshments. Please make yourself at home, and I will call in on you later to update you as to when you can meet Master Xenon." She backed out of the room with a bow.

"Where does this place remind you of?" Jann said as she looked over the cavern.

Nills stood in the center of the room and glanced over at Jann, then brought a finger to his lips before pointing at the celling.

Jann got the message: *Be careful what you say.* She nodded back.

From a pocket in his flight-suit, Nills took out a small cylindrical device, concealing this action as much as he could before flicking a switch on its face. He set it down on one of the tables.

"That should take care of any surveillance. It will disrupt any electronic devices in a ten-meter radius." He glanced around. "It reminds me of Colony Two, back in the bad old days. Same eerie vibe."

"Yeah, exactly. We've only been here a few minutes and already the place is giving me the creeps."

10

BY THE BOOK

"Have you lost you mind, Zack?" They had reconvened outside the Xenonist clearing house in Jezero, and Mia was clearly angry at his actions.

"What...I thought that was the plan? You said so —*snoop around*." Zack's exhilaration at his solo-run was now tempered by Mia's remonstrations.

"I didn't mean that you should alert them to our true intentions." Mia tapped her comms unit to flag an autonomous ground car. "I have to admit, Zack, I had you figured all wrong. I never thought you'd just rush off like that."

Zack was breathless and his face still flushed from the adrenaline coursing through his body. "Sorry, but I've been dying to get a look inside that place for ages, and when I saw the opportunity I just...I dunno...went for it. I stumbled into a hi-tech lab, lots of equipment, at least a dozen people working in there."

"We'd better not hang around here. Let's get back to the hotel." Mia grabbed his elbow and pushed him along. A few minutes later a car rolled up beside them, and they got in.

"What sort of lab was it?" Mia asked.

Zack shrugged. "What do you mean? It was just a lab."

"I mean, was it for horticulture, or bio-tech, or something else? Robotics, maybe?"

Zack thought about this for a moment, running through the memory of what he had stumbled upon when he went opening doors he shouldn't have. "Bio-lab, I think. I saw lots of those...dishes." He made a circle with his hands. "Petri dishes, and hundreds of small vials stacked row after row, and complex-looking machines, all humming and blinking."

Mia sat back in the seat. "Bio-lab, probably. But...it still doesn't mean anything."

Zack's eyes widened. "What? But of course it does. They're up to something—this proves it."

"It doesn't prove shit. They could simply be developing a better strain of cabbage." She gave Zack a look. "No law against that."

"But you saw how they reacted."

The car came to a halt right outside the hotel. "Come on." Mia gestured with her head. "Let's get a drink. I really need one after that stunt you pulled."

They exited the car, and Mia took a seat at one of the tables along the front of the hotel. The same waiter from before came out.

"What you having?" Mia jabbed a finger at a very sullen Zack.

"Water. I'm still on duty, remember?"

Mia looked up at the waiter. "Make mine a bourbon, on the rocks."

The waiter nodded his approval and sidled off. Zack resumed his sullen demeanor.

"Look, I'm not saying that everything is kosher in there." Zack's face brightened a little at this. "I'm just urging caution. It's never a good plan to jump to conclusions. All we know is that they're operating a bio-lab of some kind, nothing more."

"Then we need to go back, find out what they're really up to."

"And how do you propose we do that? Especially after your unsupervised walkabout last time. We've just given the game away."

Zack went silent and slumped back in his seat as he contemplated this conundrum. "We break in—at night, when no one's around," he finally said.

Mia threw her head back and laughed.

Zack was clearly taken aback by this reaction. "What's so funny?"

"Sorry." Mia regained some control over her mirth. "It's just you're full of surprises, Zack. I had you pegged as a *by-the-book* kind of guy. I didn't think breaking and entering was your style."

Zack shrugged and looked a little sheepish.

Mia leaned in across the table. "So what you're saying is, based simply on your hunch that *'they're up to something,'* you want to go all super-spy, break the law, and risk your job and career. Is that it?"

Zack scowled. "No. Maybe... I don't know." He shook his head. "All I'm saying is, they're up to no good."

Mia was silent for a moment as the waiter arrived with their drinks. When he left, Mia took a sip and relaxed a little. "Listen, Zack, a piece of advice. The hardest part of being a cop is not about knowing that something bad is happening. It's knowing that there's nothing you can do about it. That's the hard part. It's called the law, and it can be a pain in the ass."

Zack screwed his mouth up. "Yeah, I take your point."

"For what it's worth, I too get a bad smell from these guys. But we can't go in there all guns blazing. We need to do some solid *by-the-book* detective work. That means heading over to HQ and trolling through the archives to get a better picture of what these guys are doing. See if we can find patterns, incidents, suspicious activity, that sort of thing."

But Zack didn't answer. Instead, he yelled out in pain as something hit him on the back. He rose from the seat, gripping his right shoulder, and turned around to look back across the plaza. Mia now saw a short crossbow bolt protruding from his right shoulder.

She reacted immediately and whipped out her plasma pistol. "Zack," she shouted, "get down." She went to grab him, but two more bolts slammed into his chest. He collapsed across the table, which pitched over, sending him down on top of Mia. Another bolt slapped into the wall beside Mia's head. As she moved to put the upturned table between her and the assailant, two more bolts thudded into it.

Mia fired off two shots in the general direction just to let them know they were in for a fight. But right at that moment, the waiter came out the open door beside her.

"Get back!" she shouted, but it was too late. He was immediately hit by two bolts in quick succession. One went straight in his neck and he slumped to the floor, his eyes unblinking.

"Goddammit," Mia screamed, then tried to sneak a peek across the plaza. She spotted one assailant lying on a low rooftop opposite. She flipped the weapon to max, aimed, and fired a shot. A blot of highly charged plasma engulfed the figure; they screeched, then fell to the ground just as another crossbow bolt slammed into Mia's right foot. She yelled out in pain and ducked back behind the table.

There was another out there; the fight wasn't over yet. She crawled to the open door to the cafe, rolling the upturned table as she went to give her cover, then she quickly moved inside and sat with her back against the inner wall.

"Shit." Zack was probably dead, and so was the waiter, and there was still someone out there who wanted her dead, too.

On the floor in front of her was the shiny metal tray the waiter was using. She gripped it and used it as a mirror to see across the plaza. It was empty of people; everyone had scattered.

The tray was suddenly ripped out of her grip as a bolt hit it, and it went clattering across the floor. But it was enough—she had the location of the second attacker. Now she just needed to get a shot off. Had she been quick enough she would have fired immediately, but she hesitated, and now the attacker would have reloaded a new bolt and would be waiting for her to poke her head out. She needed a decoy.

Mia looked at the fallen waiter. He was lying part exposed in the doorway with his legs inside. Mia grabbed his trouser leg and pulled him in. He had only moved a centimeter before another bolt slammed into him. "Sorry," Mia whispered. But the attacker had taken the bait. Mia whipped around the edge of the doorway, locked on her target, and fired, just as another bolt slammed into her chest just below her left shoulder. But she heard the scream from across the street. Her shot had hit home.

Mia lay there for a while, just trying to deal with the pain. She was pretty sure there were only two attackers, and she had killed them both. All was silent, and a strange stillness filled the space around her. She saw blood pool around where she lay, and felt a little confused as to whose blood this was. She watched it for a while, mesmerized by its viscosity, the way it flowed, the way it glistened. Then her eyes began to slowly close as she slipped into darkness.

11

ENCLAVE

Around two hours after Jann and Nills were shown to their lodgings, there was a timid knock on the door. Jann rose from her seat and opened it. Anna stood outside, again flanked by the two hooded figures. "Master Xenon will see you now," she said, with a facial expression that inferred that this was an astounding privilege.

Jann glanced over at Nills. "Ready?"

He stood up and clapped his hands together. "Looking forward to it."

They were led through a series of corridors and eventually ushered into another industrial-sized elevator, except this one was highly ornate, clad with brightly patterned decorative tiles and spiraled metalwork. They rose up a level and opened out into a large, verdant biodome. Sunlight streamed through a translucent roof, infusing the space with soft, bright illumination. Tall, broad leaf plants rose up on all sides, creating dappled shadows that danced across a decorative tiled floor. The path through this foliage opened out around a circular pond with a fountain at its center. Ahead of this was a slightly raised area with low seating. A number of figures were gathered here—some sitting, some standing. They all stopped what they were doing and looked at the visitors as they approached. A tall figure broke away from a small knot of people and came forward, arms outstretched, his face a broad smile. It was Xenon Hybrid.

"Ah...there you are, Jann Malbec and Nills Langthorp. What a pleasant surprise. I couldn't believe it when they told me you were here." He strode across the space between them with purpose, and embraced Jann in a great big bearhug. She felt the air being squeezed out of her. He broke off, then turned to do the same to Nills. Xenon finally stood back and looked at them both. "To what do I owe this pleasure, after all this time?"

"Just a whim, really," Jann said, with a hint of nonchalance. "We figured we hadn't seen you in quite a while. You've become very reclusive, Xenon."

He smiled again. "True, my work has become my life. Sometimes I forget the outside world exists. But...come, come, sit and we will talk."

They moved onto the dais, and several of the hooded figures parted as Xenon ushered them to a low seating area. He sat down beside Jann along with two others as a tray of tea was brought out and placed before them on a low table. The other figures moved away and occupied another area at a respectable distance.

"You've built a substantial facility here," Jann said as she sipped the hot tea.

Xenon glanced around the verdant biodome. "Yes, we have been blessed with many newcomers all willing to offer their time and efforts to expanding the enclave."

"So why don't you use robots?" said Nills. "We had to leave ours behind in the rover."

"Our ethos here is one of simplicity—a return to nature, if you will. We believe that since we are fundamentally all products of nature, to find true internal harmony it is best to properly immerse ourselves in the natural world."

"Except you live on Mars. Hardly the natural world," said Nills, a little skeptical.

"That's where you're wrong, my friend. This planet may be harsh, unforgiving, devoid of life, but it is still a product of nature. You only have to look at the vast mountains and canyons. There is great beauty here."

"Yet to live here, we must all wrap ourselves in technology. We are forever removed from the planet by a thick layer of insulation." Jann pushed the debate.

"True, this may be so. But we try to minimize that here. We utilize only what's necessary, and robots are not necessary. They simply insulate us even further, denying us the fulfillment of our own labor. You of all people, Nills, should understand that."

"Yeah, to an extent." Nills nodded. "But I also happen

to see them as useful tools, something that augments one's own labor. In fact, I find myself getting quite attached to some, to the point where they become my friends." He gave an unapologetic gesture. "And, I doubt that any of us would be sitting here talking if it weren't for that droid that has been left abandoned out in our rover."

Xenon seemed a little confused by this answer, as if he did not quite know what Nills was referring to. "This is our way," he finally said.

"How come you never visit us in Jezero anymore?" Jann asked, changing the subject.

"My work here keeps me busy. And even though I tend not to be seen in public, more and more of the public come to see me here, and many stay."

Jann glanced around at the lush vegetation and took in the beauty of the biodome. "I can see the attraction. This place is beautiful."

"It is, and we have many more areas like this. Below us is a vast submarining horticultural complex. We have been building and expanding for a great many years, all through the labor of our followers. Many come here to seek answers, but many also stay for the peace they find from the simple agrarian life."

He swept a hand around. "What you see here is available to all in this enclave. Such a biodome is only for the rich elites in Jezero, and none exist in Syrtis—that's just an industrial hellhole." He turned to face Jann. "So, you can see the attraction. Many who arrive here have become disillusioned by the crass commercialization of

Mars. It's a source of great disappointment for them that the utopia that was promised has been corrupted so terribly. Whereas here, that dream is rekindled in them, a dream of a true enlightened civilization."

"Very laudable, Xenon. But you are forgetting that none of this can exist in isolation. Without the industries that provide the technology that insulates you from the harsh world beyond, none of this is possible," Jann said, challenging Xenon's narrative.

"The same could be said of Jezero, yet it is the playground of the elite, those who have the good fortune to insulate themselves not just from the realities of the planet, but also the grimy reality of how all this technological abundance is produced."

Jann began to realize that Xenon had changed considerably over the last few years. The Xenon she remembered was more philosophical, more into the poetry of the planet, seeking out its inherent beauty. He was more of an artist, a creative thinker, a curious eccentric. Which was why most of the citizens of Mars were happy for him to be their mascot. But now, Jann felt that the Xenon she was talking to had become harder, more cynical, less of a philosopher and more of a radical. It was troubling. She cast a glance at Nills to gauge his reactions. She knew him well enough to read his face, and it told her that he too was confused by this change in Xenon.

"It's all still a little precarious, after the destruction that the Great Storm inflicted on us," Jann replied.

"Jezero is like a ghost town, and both Syrtis and Elysium are struggling for viability. It's safe to say that the future of the colony is far from certain."

"I agree that this is a concern, but I have a feeling that we will prevail in the end."

"I don't share your optimism, Xenon. We now have a new problem on our doorstep." Jann considered that this might be a good moment to get to the point of her visit.

"Oh, and what's that?"

"A ship bound for Earth blew up on the launch pad in Jezero."

"I heard. That is most unfortunate."

"Yes. But the thing is, we found two bodies at the site with some...very strange DNA." Jann looked directly at Xenon.

"Strange? In what way?" Xenon replied as he sipped his tea.

"They were both identical, but that's not all." Jann glanced around to ensure they were not overheard and leaned in. "This DNA had elements of your own, which as you know is unique." She paused for a beat. "I just thought I'd bring it to your attention." She looked at him more intently, trying to gauge his reaction to this revelation. But she detected no apparent change in his facial expression.

"Curious," Xenon finally said, with a slight nod of his head. "Do you suspect that someone has been utilizing my DNA for some clandestine biological experiment?"

"I'm not sure what it means. I thought you might be able to shed some light on it."

Xenon sat back a little and seemed to think about this for a moment. "I see that your trip here was not simply to visit an old friend." He cocked an eyebrow at her. "But if you want my thoughts, then I think it would be very easy for someone to obtain a sample of my DNA." He picked up the teacup. "You could get it from this." He gently placed it back down on the table. "And you need to realize that my DNA has been out in the wild, so to speak, for a very long time. I've been tested and experimented on for years, so there would be samples in many of the labs both here on Mars and on Earth. Perhaps that's where you should start your search."

Jann gave a long sigh. "You're probably right, that might be the best place to start. Anyway, I just thought I'd give you a heads-up on it."

"And I thank you for that, Jann. Now"—he slapped both hands on his knees—"I do believe that food is ready to be served in the viewing area." He stood up and held out a hand. "If you'd both follow me, we have something prepared for your entertainment."

Behind them, a wide set of concertina doors were folded back, leading into yet another domed area, smaller and much less grand. But the structure was completely transparent, providing an unobstructed view of the Martian landscape. The sun sat low in the sky, just over the horizon.

"Excellent," Xenon exclaimed. "The sunset here is a

thing of great beauty, and I'm delighted you'll both be able to witness it."

They were directed over to a low, comfortable seating that arced around tables laden with food and drink. Off to one side, a group of musicians began to play. Their instruments were all acoustic—strings, wind, percussion —and all had a homemade, artisanal look to them. Yet the music they produced was ephemeral and ambient, almost hypnotic.

JANN FOUND herself relaxing as the conversations began to coalesce around the quality of food, or the sunset, or the music. Any attempt by Jann to discuss the issues facing the colony after the Great Storm were snuffed out almost immediately. In the end, she gave up and went with the flow.

Nills seemed to be enjoying himself, and regaled the assembled group with tales of his and Xenon's exploits back in the early days of the colony's founding. This gave Jann an idea. She waited for a break in the conversation.

"Do you remember that time, Xenon, when we were both trapped in that crashed shuttle we stole?"

Xenon's face struggled for a moment to recollect this incident. Then it brightened. "Yes, yes, of course. How could I forget."

Jann leaned in and directed her story to the group. "Something went wrong with the engine, and we had to crash land—it was somewhere around Gale Crater.

Anyway, we were stuck inside, couldn't get the damn door opened. I tried and tried to reroute power to the access control panel, with no luck. I thought we were going to die there." She paused for dramatic effect, and to gauge Xenon's reaction. He seemed to be enjoying the story. "Anyway, Xenon gets bored with all this, walks over to the door, and gives it a kick. And what do you know, the door simply falls off its mounts." She turned to Xenon. "You remember that?"

Xenon gave a big bright smile. "Sometimes, the simplest solutions are the best."

Everyone laughed.

THE EVENING PROGRESSED in a similar vein until Jann and Nills decided to take their leave and retire. There was much hugging and handshaking, and Anna was yet again put upon to bring them back to their lodgings. Xenon had agreed to meet them again in the morning, before they set off for the long journey back to Jezero.

When they finally entered their room and closed the door behind them, Nills put a finger to his lips, took out the jamming device, activated it, and set it down on the table. "Should be okay to talk now," he finally said.

"So, what do you think of Xenon?" Jann asked.

"I hardly recognized him. He's changed a lot—older, more cynical. It's like he's a different person."

"You know that story of the shuttle crash I was telling everyone?"

"Yeah, funny. I don't remember you mentioning that before."

"That's because it never happened."

Nills' face took on a confused look. "Never happened?"

"Yet, did you notice how Xenon remembered it?"

Nills thought about this for a moment. "Yeah, he seemed to struggle to recollect it at the start."

"That's because the person we met was not Xenon Hybrid. It's someone pretending to be him."

Nills remained silent for beat. "I...don't believe it. It can't be."

"I think the person we met was a clone. Someone who looks exactly like him, but does not have his memory. He was just pretending to remember."

"Holy shit." The reality was finally dawning on Nills. "Now that you say it, it would explain a lot."

"It does. And it also raises the question: Where's the real Xenon Hybrid?"

12

TIME TO DIG

Sound entered into Mia's consciousness—voices, some with hushed tones, some anxious, some assertive, ordering, directing. Light flickered across her retinas, blurry and indistinct. Movement—she felt her body being shifted and tugged, pushed and pulled. All these external stimuli she was only vaguely aware of. Yet as time passed, they gained more clarity, until the moment she opened her eyes and found herself in a hospital bed.

The door opened, and a medic entered. "Mia, you're awake."

Mia tried to answer, but her throat was dry and rough. It hurt just to swallow.

"Here." The medic helped her sit up and offered her some water. Mia drank it down like she had just spent five days in a desert—it felt so good. Before she'd finished, the door opened again and this time Bret Stanton and, if she wasn't mistaken, Poe Tarkin, the big MLOD boss himself, entered.

"Mia." Stanton rushed over to her. "How're you feeling?"

She handed the empty bottle of water back to the medic and looked at him. "Are you seriously asking me that question?" She swallowed hard, trying to get some feeling back into her larynx. "How would you feel if someone just tried to use *you* as a pin cushion?"

He grinned. "Good to have you back."

Mia shifted in the bed, sitting up a little more.

"We need to know what happened out there," Tarkin said in a soft, avuncular tone. "Are you able to talk about it yet?"

Mia gave a sigh, and that's when she realized her left shoulder was all bandaged up and her arm was in a sling. She jiggled her feet; they moved, that was good. But she could feel her right foot was also all bandaged up. Surprisingly, she felt no pain, only discomfort. She attributed this to the amount of painkillers that had probably been pumped into her.

"Zack?" Mia directed her question at Stanton.

"Alive, but on life support," he said gravely. "They say the next twenty-four hours will be critical."

"And the waiter?"

Stanton shook his head.

"Shit." Mia looked up at Tarkin. "Not much to tell.

One minute we were talking, drinking coffee, next it was raining crossbow bolts."

"Did you manage to get a look at the attackers?"

Mia gave him a confused look. "What do you mean? I shot both of them. Pretty sure they're dead."

Stanton looked over at Tarkin, then back at Mia. "We didn't find any other bodies."

"What? I nailed at least two of them. And I wasn't pussying around, my PEP weapon was set to max," Mia said as she slumped down a little in the bed. "Maybe they had support and cleaned up before you arrived?"

Stanton dragged over a seat, as did Tarkin. Now that she was alert, they were going to get as much out of her as they could. Not that Mia was objecting—it was good that they were taking this seriously.

"Any ideas who might have been behind this?" Stanton asked.

"Xenonists," Mia spat out.

"Xenonists?" Tarkin said with a hint of incredulity.

"Zack had a theory." Mia gave a dismissive gesture with her hand. "I know, I know. I thought it was a bit crazy, too. But he lives across the street from their HQ here in Jezero. He was keeping an eye on them, he was convinced they were up to no good. So, since I was bored sitting around waiting for flights to resume, I decided to take a stroll in there and rattle their cage. Nothing major. I planned to keep it straight, just see what reaction I got. Anyway, Zack got a rush of blood to the head and goes on a little walkabout in there, while I was distracted by the guys at reception. It was a stupid thing to do. I didn't realize the guy would be so reckless." Mia took another long drink from the water bottle.

"He managed to enter a bio-lab of some sort before we were both unceremoniously kicked out. We headed back to the hotel and bang, crossbow bolts started raining down on us."

There was silence in the room for a moment as both Stanton and Tarkin digested this story.

"Xenonists?" Tarkin finally said, this time with even more incredulity.

Mia shrugged. "Go figure."

"But they are the most benign group of people on the planet." He waved a hand around. "All they're into is... philosophy, and living the pacifist, agrarian lifestyle. Their leader is none other the Xenon Hybrid, the most revered human on Mars. It's just ludicrous to suspect them of such a well-planned hit job...ludicrous."

Mia sighed. "You may be right, Poe. It all sounds completely crazy. And that's exactly what I thought when Zack started going on about it. But the more he talked... well, I began to think there's more to these guys than they let on." She shifted again in the bed. She was becoming more alert, more restless. She wanted to get out, maybe test out her landing gear. She wanted to know what worked and what didn't. *But best not try this in front of these two, in case I end up on the floor with my ass hanging out of the hospital gown*, she thought.

"You need to go and check these guys out," she finally

said.

Tarkin shook his head. Not that he was dismissing Mia's suggestion, but that he still couldn't believe it. "Is there...anyone else you think might want you dead? An old adversary, perhaps?"

"I've gone through that list several times in my head, and nobody comes to mind that would have the wherewithal to pull a stunt like this. Hey, even you didn't believe that, Bret. Otherwise you wouldn't have given me a rookie like Zack."

Bret raised a hand. "I didn't think..."

"It doesn't matter," Mia cut him off. "It's not your fault, so don't go beating yourself up over it. Best thing for you guys to do is start digging into that Xenonist HQ and see what crawls out. I mean, there's gotta be some street camera footage of the attack, or something?"

"Nothing. No feeds. Everything was disconnected or jammed. And no eyewitnesses, at least none that are talking," said Stanton.

Poe Tarkin suddenly stood up. "I think we have imposed ourselves enough on you for the time being. It's best we leave now and let you recuperate. But rest assured, we will do everything in our power to uncover the perpetrator of this outrageous attack and bring them to justice." He glanced over at Stanton as if to say, *It's time to go.*

Mia nodded. "Good, see that you do. And take my advice—focus on the Xenonists."

Tarkin smiled, nodded, and turned to go. Stanton also

stood up and began to follow, glancing back at Mia as he did. "We'll find who was responsible, you just rest and get better." He strode out of the room.

MIA DIDN'T BELIEVE either of them. They were just trying to placate her. Sure, they would throw some resources at it, but they would be looking in the wrong direction. There was simply too strong a cognitive bias when it came to the Xenon Hybrid. No one could possibly believe that he, or his followers, were somehow a force for chaos. It was beyond comprehension. It was simply not possible. If she was going to find out the truth, then she would have to do the digging herself.

She glanced down at the floor of the room, gathered her strength, and swung her legs out over the edge of the bed. From there she slid down and planted her two feet on the ground. A sharp pain shot up through her right leg. She let out a yell, then fell flat on her face, her ass hanging out of the hospital gown.

A medic rushed in. "Ms. Sorelli, what are you doing? You shouldn't be trying to get up."

Another medic rushed in, and between them they lifted her up and sat her back on the edge of the bed.

Mia grabbed one of them by the collar. "Listen, whatever your name is, get me some crutches. I don't care if they're just sticks. I'm not staying in that bed a moment longer than I have to."

The medic was a little taken aback, but being a

professional, she simply nodded. "I will find something for you. But in the meantime, just take it easy. You don't want to injure yourself in a fall."

Mia acquiesced and shuffled herself back into the bed proper. *This is going to take a lot of work*, she thought.

13

WALKABOUT

"That's a good question, Jann," Nills said as he sat down on a low bench and leaned his back against the wall. "Are you saying that the real Xenon Hybrid is dead?"

Jann inclined her head a little. "Possibly, although we have to assume that he might also be held against his will somewhere within this enclave."

Nills sighed. "This is all messed up. If that guy up there is really a clone, then we're back to the bad old days."

"It's not something I want to contemplate, but there is no other explanation for either the new Xenon or those two guys we found at the site back in Jezero."

"But why? Why would they start doing this? After all that Xenon had been through?"

"Whatever the reason is, the answers are here

somewhere. That's why we need to take a look around—
now, while we still have a chance."

"And how do you suppose we're going to do that?
They're not going to let us just walk around."

"Can Gizmo help? Can it hack into the facility system
from inside the rover?"

Nills scratched his chin. "Possibly. Maybe it could get
us a schematic, maybe even disable some of the security."
He looked over at Jann. "Worth a shot."

He tapped the side of his temple and activated his
comms implant. A pale blue ring of light glowed around
the pupil of his right eye. "Gizmo, this is Nills. Do you
copy?"

Jann activated her own comms implant so she could
listen in.

*"Yes, Nills. I copy. How is your visit going, considering I
am here all on my own?"*

Nills looked over at Jann and rolled his eyes. "Eh,
sorry about that, buddy, but couldn't be helped. Listen, I
need you to do something for us."

Jann couldn't be sure, but she imagined she heard a
sigh from Gizmo.

"Very well, what is it?"

"You think you could gain access to this facility's
system via the rover interface link?"

There was a slight pause before Gizmo responded.
"Yes, it looks like their firewall is very rudimentary."

"Good, we need a schematic of the enclave, even if it's

just an approximation of the layout, and also which areas are consuming the most power."

"I am already working on it. But it could take some time."

"That's okay. Just let me know when you have something."

"Will do. At least now I have a job to keep me busy."

The connection terminated.

IT DIDN'T TAKE Gizmo long to come back with a schematic. Less than twenty minutes later, Jann and Nills were both looking at a 3D map of the enclave that blossomed out of a holo-slate, which Nills had fished out from a pocket. He set it face-up on one of the low tables in the room, and the two of them hunkered down to examine the map of the enclave.

The surface structures consisted of a series of domes, the largest of which was where they had met the fake Xenon. Around this were smaller domed structures that all seemed to be designated as either gardens or spaces for *'reflection.'* Then there was the docking wing for rovers on one side, with a terminal on the other side for processing goods and people arriving by shuttle. Although both these terminals were on the surface, they routed everything underground. And it was clear from the schematic that this constituted the vast majority of the facility. Possibly four times the size of what was visible on the surface.

"I had no idea it was this big," Jann said as she rotated the 3D image.

Nills pointed at the main subterranean level. "This entire sector looks to be given over to horticulture. And see here." He pointed at another level. "That's power management, with all the life support systems grouped around it. Water reclamation, oxygenator, climate control. And this level here looks to be all accommodation."

"What's this sector? Seems to be using a lot of power," Jann said as she zoomed in on yet another level of the underground enclave.

Nills tapped the area of the projection, and a data label floated above it. "Horticulture, apparently. But you're right, it's using significantly more power than these other sectors."

"Maybe it's aqua-culture or protein-culture?"

"Then why not identify it as such?" Nills looked over at Jann.

Jann stood up. "I think we should take a look."

Nills remained hunkered down, studying the diagram. "That's down two levels, and quite a distance from here. What happens if we're spotted?"

"We could plead ignorance, say we were going for a walk?"

"Hmmm...you think they'd buy that?"

"Probably not. It would be better if we can do this without alerting anybody."

Nills tapped his temple again to talk to Gizmo. "Can

you get access to any of the camera feeds on levels two and three?"

"Yes," Gizmo replied almost instantly. *"As I suspected, their firewall is virtually nonexistent. I have complete access to most of the enclave's systems."*

"Excellent. Can you route that schematic through to mine and Jann's comms units as an augmented wireframe, and give us the camera feed locations?"

"Certainly. It will take a few moments to compile. Am I correct in assuming that yourself and Jann are going on a clandestine investigation of the facility?"

"That's the plan, and we don't want to be spotted."

"Would you like me to monitor your progress and alert you to any dangers?"

"That would be great, Gizmo."

"No problem. I am happy to not be simply existing without a purpose. You should see that wireframe now."

A pale blue ring began to slightly glow around one of Jann's pupils as the retinal implant began to project the augmented reality wireframe onto her real-world vision. As she looked around the room, it was now demarcated by bright lines that scribed its dimensions. But beyond the walls, she could see the wireframe extending in all directions, fading into the distance.

"Wow," she said as she looked this way and that. "I take it all back, Nills. Reactivating Gizmo was an inspired idea."

Nills gave her one of his best grins. "I think we're all set to go walkabout."

. . .

JANN DIALED down the chromatic levels of her cloak, as did Nills. It was now a dull dark gray, almost black, absorbing most of the light that hit it. She wrapped the cloak around her and pulled the hood up over her head. All that could be seen of her face was a pale blue ring where her right eye should be. They headed out of the room, quietly walked along the corridor to the elevator, and rode it down to where the sector they wanted to investigate was located.

As they descended, Jann began to get a sense of the scale of the submarining levels from her augmented reality vision. Several camera feeds were identified, along with infrared and microwave motion sensors. They had to wait a few moments as Gizmo set about remotely disabling them. When it gave them the all clear, they exited the elevator into a wide, dimly-lit storage area. Crates and containers were piled almost to the ceiling, which was high enough to accommodate a small shuttle.

Nills pointed the way ahead, but as they moved, the roof above them began to glow with the strange bioluminescence they had seen everywhere in the facility. Jann quickly moved into the shadows. "That's not good. Can Gizmo kill the lights?"

Nills tapped his temple and mumbled some instruction to the droid. He nodded a few times, then looked over at Jann. "No can do. It's biological, not electronic. No way to shut it off."

97

Jann looked up at the celling. The illumination was fading, growing fainter. "We're probably disturbing the air flow as we move. That might be what's activating it."

"No way to hide from that. We'll be lighting up the place as we move."

Jann thought for a moment. "Yeah, but so will everyone else." She glanced up at a stack of crates. "Wait there."

She began to climb up, and scanned the entire area when she reached the top. "I can't see any other illumination. There's no one else in here." She scrambled back down. "Come on. Let's keep going."

They began to thread their way through the stacks of storage containers, and as they did, the roof overhead would illuminate their path, then dim again as they passed.

Jann suddenly stopped, then grabbed Nills' arm. "Wait up. I think there's someone else here." She pointed down toward an area where the ceiling began to glow. They froze for a moment, watching, waiting. The light was moving, coming their way, getting closer. Jann could hear voices now, nothing distinct, just some vague dialogue going on between two or possibly three people heading in their direction. She gestured to Nills to move back. They silently worked their way around the back of a large container and crouched down.

The voices seemed calm and relaxed, like a natural conversation between friends. She got the sense that they were just passing through. After a moment or two, the sound of their chatter drifted away and the ceiling light dimmed.

"We better wait here for a while and make sure those guys are far enough away not to notice us move again," Jann said as she gently sat down on the floor. They gave it five minutes before they started moving again.

As they progressed, the cavern began to narrow. Jann's augmented vision began picking out the outlines of other sectors beyond this one. "Not far now," she said as they passed into a short connecting tunnel—the far end of which was their destination.

The tunnel ended in a large steel airlock door. Nills inspected the locking mechanism, then moved over to a small control panel at the side. "Gizmo, I'm at the door to sector L3-S14, which is locked. Can you open it?"

A moment later, they heard a low whirring sound as the locking bolts retracted and the door swung open. "I love that droid," he said with a grin.

According to Jann's augmented vision, the room should be a rectangular space around three hundred meters deep by eighty meters wide, making it a sizable area, enough to accommodate several transport shuttles. It was dark, and as they entered it remained so. There was none of the overhead bioluminescence on the celling like in the cavern they had just been through.

But as her eyes adjusted to the darkness, she could see the dull outlines of several rectangular tanks, about the size of a small ground car. They gave off a faint shimmer. She reached into a pocket, fished out a flashlight, and swept it over the area. What she saw stunned her. There were rows upon rows of these tanks, hundreds of them. She moved over to one to inspect it and could see a control panel at one end, its system lights glowing in the darkness.

"Nills, look—bio-tanks." She focused her light on the side of the structure. It was transparent, filled with a dull viscous liquid, and inside floated the vague outline of a body. "Holy shit. It's a cloning tank." She looked down the length of the vast room. "They're cloning hundreds of people."

Nills remained silent.

Jann glanced over at him, concerned. "You okay?"

He nodded. "Yeah, just...memories, you know. The bad old days."

She gripped his arm. "I know. And we all thought they were over." She swept her flashlight along the side of the tank. "The Xenonists have brought all that back. This is worse that I thought, much worse."

She tapped her temple and contacted the droid. "Gizmo, are you seeing what I'm seeing?" Her ocular implant was now recording data.

"Yes Jann, I am getting visual data from both of you."

"Make sure you record all this and transmit it back to Poe Tarkin in the MLOD in Jezero. This is critically important."

"I can record everything, but I cannot transmit the data to Jezero. The rover's comms system does not have the range."

"Can you hack in and use the enclave's comms?" Nills offered.

"That might be possible, but such a data transmission would not go unnoticed. There would be no way to hide it."

"Then just record everything. We'll have to wait until we get within range of Jezero."

"We only need to get back to the waystation," Nills offered. "We can transmit from there."

"Then that will have to do." Jann terminated the connection.

THEY SPENT a while wandering through the rows of tanks, recording what they saw, trying to get a sense of the extent of the cloning operation the Xenonists had embarked on. Jann had no doubt that the two people involved in the attack on the ship at the Jezero spaceport had come from these tanks. Yet this raised more questions than it answered. Why were the Xenonists doing this? For what purpose? And how did they get access to this technology, considering it had been banned for decades?

Eventually they came to a gap in a row of tanks that ran along the side wall of the vast cavern. This gap facilitated access to a doorway, but Jann's augmented vision showed no room beyond.

Curious, she thought. "Nills, have a look at this." She pointed at the door. "Are you seeing anything on the other side of this?"

Nills stood for a moment, moving his head from side to side. "No, nothing. The schematic just ends here."

Jann tapped her temple again. "Gizmo, we're at a location approximately halfway along the right-hand side wall of the tank room. There is a door here, but no information on what's on the other side."

"Yes, I have not been able to acquire enough data on that area to create any estimate of what lies beyond."

She turned around to Nills. "What do you think?"

"You mean should we open it and take a look?" He grinned.

Jann nodded. "Yeah."

"We've come this far," Nills said as he moved over to inspect the control panel beside the door. "Looks pretty solid." He stood back, looking at the door. "Whatever's behind there, they don't want anyone just walking in."

He tapped his temple. "Gizmo, can you open that door for us?"

Again, it took the droid only a moment to bypass the security and release the locking mechanism. The door clicked open, and a crack of light broke along its edge. Nills placed a hand on it and gently pushed it inward.

It opened into a short corridor with several doors on either side, one of which was open and seemed to be the main source of the light. They silently entered, careful not to make a noise. Slowly edging their way to the light.

Jann peered around the edge of the doorway. It was someone's living quarters. The walls were arranged with shelves stacked with old-fashioned books and papers. Art hung from the walls and strange antique science instruments were arrayed on various tables. The entire scene was like something from another century. She slowly moved her head around the edge of the doorway, trying to see more of the room.

An old holo-table desk came into view, cluttered with papers and junk. Sitting behind the desk was a man, writing something by hand, his long hair obscured his face. He somehow sensed their presence, jerked his head up, and looked directly at Jann.

It was Xenon Hybrid.

14

A PROMISE

It didn't take Mia long to figure out how to walk again. The crossbow bolt that went through her foot had only pierced the outside edge. No major damage, just very painful. So with the aid of a crutch and a handful of painkillers, she was up and about. Her shoulder, however, had suffered a lot more damage, and she had to keep her arm in a sling so as not to start it bleeding again. Nevertheless, thirty hours after she woke up in the hospital, Mia Sorelli hobbled in to visit Zack in the intensive care unit.

The doctors had given her five minutes, no more. He had survived the first twenty-four hours, but he was still critical. Two officers stood on guard outside the intensive care unit, along with a mean-looking security droid.

She sat down on the edge of the bed and gently held his hand, felt its warmth, felt its lifeforce. "You hang in there, buddy. Don't give up. And trust me when I say that

I will find the bastards responsible. I'm not leaving this planet until I do."

She sat for a moment in silence, nothing but the hum of machines and the wheeze of the ventilator. She nodded to him. "Gotta go, Zack. They've got me on a tight leash. Anyway, like I said, I got work to do—for both of us." She stood up and hobbled out of the room.

Her next port of call was Bret Stanton's office. She had tried a few times to contact him, but got the feeling she was being fobbed off. So, she decided to just walk right on in there and find out if they had searched the Xenonist clearing house in Jezero yet, and if so, what they had found.

Yet simple as this all sounded—to just walk right in there—Mia had a few practical problems to deal with, not least the fact that walking was a painful experience. Also, like Zack, they had stationed two officers and security droids to keep her safe, and their interpretation of that directive was to keep her contained in the hospital. But they clearly didn't know Mia Sorelli. If she wanted to go see Bret Stanton, then there was nothing they could do to stop her except to physically restrain her. And since that was not an option, they had no choice other than to follow along after her.

So less than twenty minutes after leaving the hospital, Mia hobbled into MLOD HQ and barged into Bret Stanton's office.

"Mia, what the hell?" Stanton almost jumped when

he saw her. "You're supposed to be in the hospital, getting well again."

"I'm fine."

"You can't come barging in here just like that."

"Oh, and why not?"

"Because...because you just can't."

"Relax, Bret. You'll pop a vein."

Stanton rubbed his forehead and sighed. "Why do I bother." He gave another sigh, deeper this time, then sat back down behind his desk.

"You've been fobbing me off, Bret. So I'm here to find out what's been going down."

"Mia." Bret's voice was calm, almost avuncular. "You have to realize you're not part of the department anymore. You've just got to accept that. You're a Mars envoy, you're in State. In fact, you should be halfway to Earth by now."

"Except, someone tried to kill me...twice. And I'd like to know what you're doing about it."

"We're doing everything in our power to get to the bottom of this." Bret leaned back in his seat. "You know that, Mia."

"Have you searched the clearing house yet?"

Bret leaned his head slightly to one side and screwed his mouth up. "It's tricky."

"You mean you haven't?"

"There's a lot of...politics involved. You have to realize that these guys have a lot of friends in high places." He jabbed a finger upward. "A lot of the Council are old pioneers, original colonists. They see the Xenonists as...a cultural institution. They're reluctant to go in all guns blazing."

"What, in case they upset them?"

"Partly, and partly because of the social repercussions that would inevitably occur should the pure, wholesome, ethical reputation of the Xenonists be shattered and revealed to be a lie. This, coming after the trauma of the Great Storm, would be devastating to the morale of the people."

"So we do nothing, is that what you're saying?"

"No, I'm not saying that, Mia. I'm just saying we need to tread lightly. But rest assured, we will get the answers."

Mia slumped down into a seat. Her shoulder was aching and her body felt tired. "I dropped in on Zack."

"How is he?"

"Still alive, just about. But I made him a promise."

Staunton gave Mia a suspicious look. "Oh?"

"Yeah, I promised him I would not leave Mars until I found who was responsible."

"You should leave that to us, Mia."

Mia looked at herself, examining her foot and her shoulder. "Well, I'm not up to much, as you can see. But I still want to do a little digging into archives, look into this cult, see what the history is. So, you can do me a favor and set me up with a terminal and some space to work."

Bret shook his head. "And how do I explain that to the Council?"

"You're forgetting I'm an envoy, off to represent

Martian interests back on Earth. As part of my job, I need to be up to speed on the current socioeconomic status of the colony." She gave him a wry smile.

Bret was silent for a moment, then he leaned in over his desk and pointed at her. "Just don't get me into trouble, okay?"

"Can't promise that."

"Okay, but if you dig anything up, please come to me with it. At least give me a chance to cover my ass."

Mia nodded. "Deal."

They sat for a moment in silence before Mia finally spoke again. "You know, Bret, you've come a long way since that time on the caravan to Syrtis when I was the one urging caution."

Bret gave a laugh. "Yes, I suppose I have. But then again, I did have a very good teacher."

15

INNERMOST CAVERN

Xenon's eyes flicked from Jann, to Nills, and back. A tense silence permeated the room for a moment, like a taut bow. Then Xenon's face slowly morphed into a look of recognition, quickly followed by confusion. His mouth opened slowly as if his brain struggled to formulate some words.

"Jann...Nills?" he finally said. "Is it...really you? How...how did you get in here?"

"We traveled all the way up to the enclave to see you. But when we arrived, we were met by someone who is trying to pass himself off as you," Jann said as she stepped closer and studied his face. "So we went searching."

Xenon's eyes now flicked over to the open doorway. "They will know you're here, they will come. You must get out."

He stood up quickly, brushed past them, and went to

the doorway. He looked down along the corridor. "The door is open. How did you get in?" Yet before they could answer, he waved a hand. "It doesn't matter. You must get out, they will know."

He looked over at Jann and Nills. "Argon, he's the one you probably met. An interloper, a radical, and very dangerous." Xenon glanced around the room. "He's the one who locked me up in this place, him and his followers. I've been incarcerated here for...I don't know how long."

"Come with us, we'll get you out of here," Nills said as he moved over to stand beside his old friend.

Xenon hesitated.

"It'll be okay," said Jann. "We'll get you back to Jezero City. They need to know what's going on here."

Nills tapped his temple. "Gizmo, get the rover ready. We're leaving, and we have Xenon with us."

But Xenon seemed to have difficulty processing this sudden development, not sure if what he was seeing was real, that his old friends were truly standing right in front of him, that escape was possible.

"Xenon, we gotta go. Time to move," Jann urged.

He nodded, then cast one last look at the room before they headed out into the vast cloning cavern beyond.

Xenon gave an audible gasp when he saw the tanks. "My god, they're producing hundreds."

"What happened here, Xenon? How did it come to this?" Jann said as they threaded their way through the rows of tanks.

Xenon sighed. "Many years ago, new people started coming to the enclave. People with radical ideas. Militants, extremists."

"What sort of ideas?" Jann continued.

"They wanted a better Mars populated by a new, pure race—Homo ares. Fundamentally, they wanted a Mars only for those who were born here, even advocating for the expulsion of all Earthlings. I tried to reason with them, of course. Then tried to fight them. But I was naive. In the end, they took over and started to execute their ultimate plan. Yet they still needed me—as a figurehead, I suppose—so they effectively imprisoned me in that place since...before the Great Storm, I think."

"But why the cloning?" Jann asked. "Why start that again after all that had happened?"

"Breeding. The originals were depleted and can't reproduce, so the only way to reestablish a new bloodline was through cloning. You must understand that Argon and his followers see themselves as a superior race, a more advanced human, and the true inheritors of Mars. They see people from Earth as just here to exploit the citizens and resources, like the old European colonists of centuries past."

Jann stopped dead in her tracks and looked at Xenon. "Wait a minute, are you saying they're planning a takeover?"

Xenon gave her a careful look. "As far as I can tell, yes."

"Holy shit. This is insane."

"Jann, Xenon, hold up." Nills raised one hand in the air and touched his temple with the other. "We've got company."

"I knew they'd find us," Xenon said with an air of fatality.

Nills jerked his head this way and that as he analyzed the data entering his augmented vision. "Two groups, one moving through the far cavern." He swung around, gesturing toward the back of the tank room. "Another coming from somewhere behind us."

"Do we need to go through the cavern? Is that our only way out?" Jann said as she began to study her own augmented vision.

"Gizmo, can you find us an alternate route?" Nills concentrated for a moment as the droid did the calculations.

"I know another way," said Xenon. "Follow me."

They started moving toward the right-hand side of the vast cloning cavern, then followed along the side wall, heading for the same entrance that Jann and Nills had used to gain access. But before they reached it, Xenon directed them into a narrow side passage that was almost completely hidden in the darkness. From there, they mounted a rickety metal stairway that looked as if it might collapse at any moment, spacing themselves out so as not to put too much weight on it. It clanged with every step, the sound reverberating throughout the facility.

Eventually, they arrived at ground level. The stairway ended in a broad landing with several doors, one of which would lead them directly into the rover docking wing. Nills stood and inspected it, using his augmented vision to see beyond.

"What is it?" Jann asked.

"There's two guards hanging around outside the entrance to the docking wing. Check your AR." He pointed at his eye.

Jann looked at the door and focused on the augmented wireframe extending out on all sides. In one sector, she could see a label for a camera feed. She extended her arm and gestured at it with her hand. The camera feed zoomed out, and she could see a fisheye view of the rover docking area. Two Xenonists were positioned right in front of the tunnel entrance.

"We should try and take them. There's only two," she whispered to Nills.

A loud clang reverberated up the stairwell from down below.

"Sounds like we don't have a choice, they're closing in," said Nills. "Xenon, you stay put."

He gently opened the door a crack and peered through, then whispered, "Dead ahead, around ten meters."

Jann steeled herself and nodded. "Okay, let's do it."

"On three...two...one." Nills flung the door wide open, and they charged across the space, slamming into the two hapless guards before they could react. Jann swung a kick into the back of the guard's knees, and he dropped like a marionette with its strings cut. She leapt high into the air and landed her knee down on his chest, knocking the wind out of him. Finally, she reached down and pulled the plasma pistol from his waistband, checked it was set on stun, stood up, and blasted him with it.

She turned to see that Nills had also managed to incapacitate the other guard and was now relieving him of his plasma weapon.

"Xenon, come. Hurry," Jann called out.

He was still standing in the doorway, looking back at the stairway they had just climbed. "They're right behind us," he said as he rushed over to Jann and Nills.

"Let's go." Nills hefted the weapon and advanced down the docking tunnel. But he'd only moved a few steps when two incandescent balls of plasma came streaking out from the darkness beyond. One hit Nills on the chest, and the second slammed into Xenon's shoulder.

Jann instinctively dropped to the floor and managed to get a shot off. The bright ball of energy briefly illuminated the darkened tunnel, and she caught a glimpse of several Xenonists in the distance.

She kept low and crawled over to Nills. He was slumped on the floor, his back against the wall, holding his chest and grimacing in agony. Xenon was no better. "Goddammit," said Jann as she fired off two more shots. But she was shooting blind, just buying some time.

"Give it up," a voice shouted out from the darkness of the tunnel. "You're surrounded, there's no way out." With that, Jann could hear the clamor behind her as the other group came rushing up the stairwell and gathered around the doorway. They took a moment to assess the situation, then slowly advanced.

Jann was trapped. She couldn't shoot her way out, so she slowly lowered the weapon to the floor and raised one hand while quickly touching her temple with the other. "Gizmo, get out now! Bring the data to the MLOD, to Poe Tarkin..." A bolt of plasma slammed into her chest, sending her entire body into spasms. Her vision blurred, she lost control of her muscles, and consciousness slipped away from her.

16

PRIMARY DIRECTIVE

Gizmo considered the audiovisual data streaming into it via the camera feeds in the docking area. Both Nills and Jann had been rendered inoperable and lay slumped on the floor of the tunnel. The other human, Xenon, was similarly incapacitated.

It probed the ocular implants for both Nills and Jann, but there was no response. The high-energy plasma blasts they had been subjected to had fried the circuitry. It also meant that the droid had no way to ascertain their current state of health, or even if they were already dead.

Its last directive from Jann had been to disengage the rover, make its way back to Jezero City, and present the data that they had collected to Poe Tarkin, the head of the MLOD. Yet, from somewhere deep inside its silicon brain, a secondary directive emerged—one that would not fundamentally countermand the primary. So, it ran the numbers, considered the possibilities, estimated the odds. It searched for any possible scenario where it could effect a rescue of the three humans that currently lay scattered on the floor of the rover docking tunnel.

It was still hacked into the enclave via the rover docking interface and maintained some control over many of the internal systems. One possibility it considered was to close the emergency depressurization door at the far end of the tunnel, isolating the docking wing from the rest of the facility. But that would still leave four well-armed guards to deal with. And while the droid could take a lot more damage from a plasma weapon than a human, it knew only too well that it was not invulnerable. Also, it had no weapons of its own to fight back with.

To rescue any of the humans would mean opening the airlock door, entering the tunnel, and dragging them one by one back into the rover, all while under a sustained attack. It was not possible. Probability of success—approximately zero. And even that window of opportunity was closing, as both Nills and Jann were being dragged out of the docking tunnel and into the main facility. With all other options exhausted, it finally made the decision to abandon them and follow the primary directive from Jann—it would make a run for Jezero City.

Gizmo powered up the rover and instigated the undocking procedure. But it failed to disengage; the system had been manually overridden, it could not get free. To add to the droid's woes, it detected two other rovers preparing to undock, presumable to block its progress should it figure out a way to break free. It didn't have much time.

Again, it analyzed the situation and considered the options. It could not release the locking bolts holding the rover tight to the docking port. But that's not to say it was completely trapped—it could simply use brute force. The rover was powered by a micro-fusion reactor feeding an electric drive train. That gave the rover a huge amount of torque.

Gizmo carefully monitored the activity inside the tunnel, and when Jann, Nills, and Xenon were finally dragged back into the main facility, past the emergency depressurization airlock, it put the metaphorical pedal to the metal and applied full power to all six wheels.

Great clouds of dust and sand billowed up all around the machine as the tires fought for traction. The rear airlock docking port creaked and cracked as the forces on it started to undermine its integrity. Under normal circumstances, no one in their right mind would consider doing something like this because the result would be cataclysmic depressurization and almost certain death. But Gizmo, being a robot, had no such concern. Therefore, it kept the power dialed up to eleven.

The rover began to swerve from side to side as the wheels spun in the dirt. A broad crack appeared along the outer edge of the docking port, and cabin pressure dropped dramatically as the air evacuated. Finally, the entire port tore away from the main structure and the rover broke free. It shot forward like a missile and slammed straight into the side of one of the rovers trying to block its path. But the sheer momentum of the machine's escape velocity made short work of the obstruction, and sent the other rover spinning and tumbling across the dusty surface.

By now, the cockpit was a sea of screeching alerts and flashing lights. Most of the windshield was gone, and the rear was a tail of torn metal and flailing wires. Yet Gizmo pushed the machine to the maximum, leaving a trail of billowing dust in its wake. But this freedom didn't last long, because a second rover was now hot on Gizmo's tail and gaining fast.

The droid analyzed the rover's drive systems, hoping to squeeze more speed, but it was designed as a workhorse rather than a racehorse. Gizmo overrode the safety systems, allowing the drive motors to suck in more energy. But more energy meant more heat, and more alerts started flashing as the drive system temperature rose beyond critical.

Gizmo scanned the terrain, looking for a more rugged surface. It was something that might give it the edge because it could not outrun its pursuers on the flat. It changed course, swinging wide, aiming for a rocky patch around a kilometer to the southeast. Here, the ground was cracked and broken, with boulders scattered about. If it could make it there, then it had a chance. Gizmo risked a little more juice to the drive, pushing the envelope, trying to maintain a lead.

It was half a klick from the change in terrain when an incandescent ball of plasma slammed into the rear of the rover. The power systems died momentarily and the high-energy electrical spike overloaded the circuitry, but Gizmo coaxed it back to life, shutting down unnecessary subsystems. The rover's drive reengaged, and it raced into more challenging terrain.

But the pursuers had gained significantly, and two more plasma bolts slammed into the rover. This time the power failed completely, and nothing Gizmo could do would bring it back. The droid finally lost control, the rover veered awkwardly, hit a rocky embankment, and took off high in the Martian air. It spun violently as it flew, and Gizmo found itself being thrown out through the nonexistent windshield. It arced through the thin Martian atmosphere in a near perfect parabola before finally impacting the surface into deep, soft sand some distance away, and ending up almost completely buried.

Farther behind, the rover finally hit the ground, but it was less fortunate than the droid as it slammed down onto hard rock. It bounced and tumbled, bits flying off in all directions, then finally exploded in a fiery ball of uncontained plasma as the fusion reactor disintegrated.

17

ACCESS DENIED

For a cult that supposedly eschewed technology, the Xenonists seemed to acquire a lot of sophisticated equipment. This was the conclusion that Mia was slowly coming to as she spent more and more time looking into their past activities.

Long before the Great Storm, around the time of the decennial celebrations, Xenon Hybrid was little more than a one-man cult. He had no followers as such, just admirers. And although he had been elected president of Mars by a unanimous Council vote some time earlier, no one really took it seriously. He might as well have been president of the Jezero Horticultural Society. In fact, one could argue that the latter had more power.

Yet, it was around this time that Xenon stopped his wandering and settled down in an old, isolated research station up in the Plains of Utopia, which had been donated to him by the Martian state. Mia started her investigations at this point in time, as this was when people began to visit the enclave hoping to talk with Xenon and seek his wisdom. Yet some of these visitors never came back, choosing instead to remain and create the foundation of the enclave it would later become.

But not all who took the trip to seek Xenon's counsel were citizens of Mars. Some traveled from as far away as Earth. And as Mia scanned the lists of these intrepid pilgrims that passed through Jezero on their way to the enclave, several names stood out. Names of people who were clearly representatives of various Earth-based corporations—no doubt looking to gain some traction with the Xenonists.

But one name stood out more than most, and that was none other than Orban Dent, Montecristo Industry's old head of security. It was someone Mia had history with. A nasty individual who would do pretty much anything for a buck. But in many ways, it was not that surprising. During the Great Storm there was a supposed embargo on shipments from Earth, and anything that did come in was routed through Montecristo—they had almost a complete monopoly. Therefore, if you wanted something you had to deal with them. Yet Orban Dent was something of a lone wolf, a fixer, a facilitator, as well as a gun for hire. If his name was on something, you pretty much knew it was highly suspect.

It was not long after these visits that a big increase in shipments started to wend their way up to the enclave. More money seemed to be available, and it rapidly grew in both wealth and size. Some of these supplies were what one might expect for a growing colony: building materials, machines for soil processing, atmosphere processing, power generation, and so on. But others were clearly the type of equipment that would only be utilized by a bio-lab. DNA sequencers, centrifuges, microscopes.

All this equipment was routed through the port in Jezero, and it was these records that Mia spent her time perusing from a lonely desk in a dark and pokey corner of the MLOD HQ.

Stanton, to his credit, let her have her way. But it was under the proviso that she didn't go meddling in the ongoing investigation. Mia agreed—she had no choice. She also got the impression that Stanton felt he could at least keep an eye on her here, and there was less likelihood that another attempt would be made on her life within these walls.

It had taken her less than a sol to get this far. She had also moved into a small accommodation module on one of the upper floors of HQ and was beginning to feel physically better. She could walk again without the aid of a crutch, and could take her arm out of the sling for short periods. She had also dropped in to see Zack again, who was still on life support, but the doctors spoke in less fatalistic tones—a good sign, she presumed.

By sol two of her investigations, she began to get a better understanding of the evolution of the Xenonists. While the Great Storm had almost brought the rest of Mars's society to its knees, the Xenonists came out of this period with a renewed strength and vigor. They had built up their resources before the storm, like a caterpillar building its chrysalis. And so when the storm ended, a whole new creature emerged. They became more politically active, setting up new enclaves and spreading more propaganda. Ultimately, they were given a lot of leeway to expand by both the regular citizens and the authorities, since most viewed them as a benign cultural institution.

So, who was funding all this expansion? To get some insight into this, Mia focused her attention back on the shipping manifests, the documentation giving the exact details of all shipments coming into the port in Jezero. And this was when Mia's investigations began to run into roadblocks. Public information on them started to dry up, and she had difficulty tracking down any documentation regarding their trade activities.

But what really piqued her interest was a number of supply ships from Earth that had their manifest documentation restricted. Any time she tried to access this information, she was met with an *access denied* notice. And even as a Mars envoy, she did not have the clearance. Questions started accumulating in Mia's head. What exactly were they bringing in that required such secrecy? Were these supplies bound for the Xenonists? Who authorized this? She needed answers, so she stood up from her desk and hobbled off to find Stanton.

. . .

MIA STRODE into his office while he was taking a call and slid her slate across his desk. "Take a look at this," she said, without waiting for him to finish.

He glanced at her, then at the slate screen, then resumed his call. "Eh...let me get back to you on that," he said, to whomever it was on the other end of the line, and terminated the conversation.

He leaned back in his chair and gave Mia a long, hard look. "Any chance you could let me know when you're coming, maybe even knock once in a while?"

Mia ignored him and pointed at the slate. "Take a look."

Stanton gave a defeated sigh and again glanced down at the screen for a moment, before looking back up at Mia with raised eyebrows. "This is a classified database you're trying to access."

"Correct. It's the import manifest of a select number of supply landings just after the Great Storm."

"So?" Stanton replied, a little annoyed.

"So why is it classified?"

Stanton gave her a considered look. "I don't know. But what's it got to do with anything?"

"You remember Orban Dent?"

Stanton raised his eyebrows. "Yeah. But I thought he'd disappeared."

"He did. But from what I'm seeing here, he was into a lot more than we imagined at the time. My guess is that when his backers were trying to gain influence here on Mars, they spread their net far and wide. One of the targets was Xenon and his followers. No doubt they saw them as a group that could be infiltrated. So, before the Great Storm, he made several visits to their enclave up north. Then a short while later, shipments from Earth began to arrive." Mia pointed to several lines on the screen. "The volume dropped off as Earth began their embargo, but resumed again once we were out of the worst of it." Mia took back the slate, tapped a few icons, and handed it back to Bret.

"See here, this is the manifest for one of the earlier shipments. There's a lot of bio-tech equipment on that list. I ran it by a contact over in forensics, and he reckons it could be used for developing new plant species or bacteria, but it's grossly over-specified for your average botanist. In other words, they don't need this type of advanced tech to engineer a better potato."

Stanton remained silent, studying the screen, digesting the information, rubbing his bottom lip, thinking. "We did a search of the clearing house in Jezero," he finally said, matter-of-factly.

"And?"

"And we found nothing of interest."

"Did you do a proper search?"

"You mean did we unscrew every access panel and crawl through every duct in the entire sector? No. But there was no lab in there."

"Zack saw a lab, quite a sophisticated one."

"Well, unfortunately he's in an induced coma in an

intensive care unit. And even if he wasn't, it's just his word against..." Stanton's sentence trailed off.

"Against who?"

Stanton leaned back in his seat and sighed. "We got an ear-bashing from the Pioneer sector on the Council for doing a search of the clearing house. They see it as an insult to the legacy of the colony founders."

"The Xenonists are hiding something, Bret. I can smell it. I need to find out what's in those manifests."

"Sorry, I can't get access to this." He gestured at the tab. "It's above my pay grade."

"What about the chief, Poe Tarkin?"

"Doubt it. This would require approval from the Council, and since we've just pissed off the Pioneers with that search, well..." He shrugged.

They were silent for a beat. Mia mulled over her options. If this rabbit hole she was going down led all the way to the Council, then she would be entering very choppy waters. It was a cesspit of factions and intrigue, way beyond Mia's ability to navigate. Yet, there was one person she could trust—one who could swim in those waters like a well-oiled barracuda.

Mia leaned over and picked the slate off the desk. "It's okay, Bret. I get the picture."

"Sorry I can't help." His reply seemed genuine.

Mia gave a nod.

"So, what are you going to do? Are you taking it to the chief?"

"No, I'm taken it to Dr. Jann Malbec."

"Malbec?" Stanton almost shouted. "Have you not heard?"

Mia stopped and looked back. "Heard what?"

"She's gone AWOL. Her and Langthorp headed off into the lowlands in an old transport rover."

"How long ago was this?"

"A few sols ago, three or four maybe."

Mia sighed and deflated slightly. "Any way to contact her?"

"No, they've gone incommunicado. Even the rover's tracking beacon is off."

"Well, that's just great."

"On the upside, you'll be happy to hear that Langthorp rescued that droid of yours from the museum."

"Gizmo?"

"Yeah, that's the one. Council is mighty pissed off about that, too."

Mia pondered this for a moment, then shrugged. "Okay, well thanks for the heads-up." And again she turned to go.

"I wouldn't fret about it, Mia. Just stay safe for the next few sols, until flights resume. Then you can get off this rock and back to Earth—home-free."

"Home-free, yeah. Well, I still have one last thing I need to do."

"And what's that?"

"The only thing left to do, Bret. I'm going to get drunk," Mia said, then hobbled out of the office.

18

SHOULDER TO SHOULDER

Jann anxiously watched over Nills as he drifted in and out of consciousness. He lay flat on his back on a low makeshift bed, his breathing labored. He had sustained a direct hit on the chest from a high-energy plasma blast, just below his right shoulder. It was burned and scarred, and the impact site had a dull purple color indicative of internal bleeding. He would need treatment, and soon, otherwise he could die. Her own injuries, and Xenon's, were insignificant by comparison; they had simply been stunned, nothing life threatening—unlike Nills.

Jann had regained consciousness a few hours earlier and found herself in a sparsely furnished, nondescript room, around ten meters square. There was only one door into it, a steel slab with no discernible handle.

Xenon was sitting cross-legged on the floor beside her, mute. He had said very little since she awoke.

Perhaps the realization that he may never taste freedom again was too much for him. Although, Jann was never sure what went on in his head.

Her mind turned to Gizmo. She comforted herself with the thought that there was a chance the droid had escaped, and had somehow manage to transmit the data that she and Nills had collected back to MLOD in Jezero. If so, then agents would be here soon to put an end to this insanity. She clutched Nills' hand. "Hang in there, help is on the way."

The door opened, and three well-armed Xenonist guards strode in followed by Argon. This incursion finally evoked a reaction from Xenon. He opened his eyes, uncrossed his legs, and stood up. From his body language, Jann thought he was about to physically attack Argon. But he relaxed, moved over to the farthest corner of the room, and sat down again on a low bench.

Argon flicked a glance at him, then looked down at Nills. "Unfortunate," he said, shaking his head a little. "Most unfortunate," he repeated. "It seems that one of our security personnel was a little reckless with his weapon settings, and Langthorp has borne the brunt of that."

"He needs medical help," Jann said, now standing directly in front of Argon.

He waved a hand. "Yes he does, and we can discuss that in a moment. But first I have some news for you." Argon paused as he took a seat on a low stool facing Jann, while keeping Xenon visible in his periphery. "Your rover has been destroyed, and your droid along with it. It suffered a reactor breach and was instantly vaporized. All that remains is a blackened crater."

Gizmo gone? Jann thought. She fought to not reveal her reaction, not wanting to give Argon the satisfaction.

"I can understand that this will come as a blow to you," Argon said almost sympathetically. "We intercepted it not far from here, so none of the data you collected on your clandestine walkabout was transmitted back to the MLOD in Jezero." He gave her a serious look. "I believe this was your intention?"

Jann remained stony-faced.

"It has also come to our attention that neither you nor Nills saw fit to inform anyone of your visit here. Rather remiss of you, don't you think?" He sat back a little on the stool and adjusted his robe. "No one knows you're here. And when they do eventually go looking for you, all they'll find is the charred remains of your rover and assume that both you and Langthorp were incinerated along with it. An unfortunate accident— nothing more." He gave a theatrical gesture with his hand.

"So, my point is this. No one is coming to look for you —at least not here. You are on your own now."

"You can't keep us here, Argon," Jann said finally. "You don't seem to realize who you're dealing with."

"Quite the contrary. It's because of who you are that you're still alive and not being recycled at this very moment."

Jann inclined her head toward the semiconscious Nills. "He urgently needs medical treatment."

"As I said, this is possible. But first we would require your cooperation with our...vision."

"Vision? What's that supposed to mean?"

"Don't listen to him, Jann," Xenon said, suddenly getting to his feet.

The guards instantly raised their weapons at him. Argon seemed unperturbed and casually adjusted his cloak again, flicking some dust from the sleeve. "You had your chance, Xenon. And you made your decision a long time ago."

"What? To endorse your insanity?" Xenon snapped back.

"You still fail to realize that you are no longer relevant."

Jann could see that this spat was just wasting time, and Nills didn't have any to spare. "What vision?" she asked.

Argon readjusted his focus back on her. "Someone of your standing in the Martian community could be of great help to us. There are many of us here who have nothing but the highest respect for your enormous contribution to the foundation of this colony, and that of Langthorp, of course. This is why we would like to see you as part of the next phase in the evolution of human civilization here on the planet."

"By the next phase, I assume you mean cloning?"

"That's part of it, yes. But you must see what is

happening to our society? Those of us who consider ourselves true Martians are being cast aside, turned into second-class citizens as the planet is handed over to people who seek only to exploit it for profit."

"It's called economics, Argon. We don't survive without it."

"Ahh, but that's where you're wrong. We believe that not only can we survive without it, but we can prosper. We intend to create a new and different society with an enlightened population of true Martians. An evolutionary step forward for humanity, a society far superior than any that Earth has to offer."

"Let me guess, that's where the clones come in."

"Like I said, that's only part of it. We're talking about giving Mars back to those who founded this colony: the originals, the pioneers. And from that cohort, we can build anew."

"So, what do you want from me and Nills?" Jann gestured at the injured engineer.

"You are both part of this cohort. Stand shoulder to shoulder with us as we move into this new era on Mars."

"And if we don't?"

"Then you're simply part of the problem, not the solution. You will have negated your right to exist, and you will be recycled." With this pronouncement, Argon stood up and signaled to his security contingent that he was ready to leave.

"I will give you a little time to consider your future path. But be aware that we'll soon be entering the next phase. You have twenty-four hours to decide." He strode out of the room, and his entourage followed.

"Next phase? What the hell does that mean?" Jann turned to Xenon, who had sat back down on the bench, resting his arms across his knees.

"I'm not sure, but I do know they have some master plan—and cloning is only part of it. Clearly, they must realize that they can't keep producing more and more clones. It will not go unnoticed. There's something bigger at play here, but what that might be I have failed to imagine."

"But it doesn't make any sense." Jann shook her head. "*Shoulder to shoulder*, what does that mean? As soon as we do that, then we'll be announcing our existence, that we're alive and well, and the truth will come out. How does that help the Argon and his followers?"

"There is something else going on," said Xenon. "Something we do not yet see."

Jann sat down beside Nills again and remained silent while she considered their situation. Finally, she turned back to Xenon. "If Gizmo has been destroyed, then Argon is right, no one is coming. We are on our own. If Nills is to be saved, then I have no option but to go along with Argon's request."

Xenon raised his head to look back at her. "I understand, Jann. You must do what needs to be done. But I am not one to be giving advice. I've been a fool—worse, a coward, hiding in my cell while my legacy is destroyed. But no more. Be warned, Jann Malbec, the first opportunity I get to kill Argon, I will take without hesitation or care for my own safety."

Jann looked back at Xenon for a moment. His body was tense, his fists clenched, and she did not doubt his intentions. "I sincerely hope you get that chance," she said with a nod.

19

DECISION FORK

When Gizmo finally impacted the Martian surface, having been unceremoniously ejected from the disintegrating rover, it immediately performed a diagnostics routine to assess the damage to its systems—fortunately, it was minimal. Nothing more than a damaged comms antenna. After satisfying itself of its operational capabilities, it took stock of its surroundings.

The droid was buried deep in a sand pit, with just its main sensor array poking out. But it was enough for it to do a full 360-degree scan of the surrounding area. Off in the distance, approximately seven hundred meters away, it observed three humans in EVA suits examining the wreckage of the rover. Not that there was much to see, since the energy released from the fractured fusion reactor vaporized most of it. Now, all that remained was a charred, blackened crater.

The three figures examined the site for a short while. Then, seemingly satisfied that nothing was left of the droid that had been operating the runaway machine, they gradually returned to their own transport and headed back in the direction of the enclave. When all that could be seen of their rover was a distant trail of dust, Gizmo extracted itself from its sandy pit. It spun its tracks a few times to shake off the dust, then scanned the horizon again—and considered its options.

Its primary directive was to get the data that Jann and Nills had acquired into the hands of Poe Tarkin back in Jezero. It could head for the waystation under its own power and transmit from there. But that was a very long way to travel for a small droid such as Gizmo, and it was unlikely it could make it that far under its own power. Gizmo then swung its sensor array back toward the direction it had just come from and scanned the horizon. The pursuers were long gone, and it could detect no activity for several kilometers.

With no ability to get to the waystation, Gizmo calculated that it had no choice but to head back to the enclave. If it could make it there, then it may have a few better options. So, with the sun setting in the west, Gizmo powered up its motors and set off across the dusty Martian landscape.

IT WAS some hours later when the droid finally arrived on the periphery of the enclave. Having hacked its security systems earlier for Nills, it knew that the facility had motion sensors set up to detect any movement up to approximately two kilometers around the perimeter. If it got any closer it would be detected, so it decided to wait and hitch a ride.

Off to one side of the main track, it took cover behind a mound of regolith, tall enough for it to conceal itself and not be seen by any approaching traffic. It settled down and waited for what could be a long time.

Hours passed, the sun had long set, and overhead the night sky sparkled with the faint light from an infinity of stars. Only one rover had passed along the main track since Gizmo set up camp, but that was heading in the wrong direction, leaving the facility, not entering. Shortly after that a shadow passed overhead, blocking out a patch of stars. Gizmo scanned the object and concluded it was a small transport shuttle. It tracked it as it slowed, came to a hover on the far side of the facility, and disappeared behind the primary dome as it came in to land.

Nothing else happened for a few more hours, and soon dawn would be breaking over the horizon to the east. But Gizmo became alerted again, this time from the south. As it scanned the track, off in the distance it could sense the flicker of rover headlamps as it bounced along the road. Gizmo gauged its speed and calculated it would be here in six minutes and forty-two seconds. It reoriented itself behind the mound to ensure the best purchase for its tracked wheels. It would need to move fast to catch this rover.

Fortunately, the rover slowed down a little now that it was nearing the facility, and as it passed, Gizmo accelerated out from behind its hiding place and raced after it, grabbing onto a hand-hold on the rear and pulling itself up. It clung to the back of the machine, bouncing along toward the enclave.

As the rover approached and began to reorient itself for docking, Gizmo released its grip, dropped back onto the ground, and headed for the far end of the docking wing. It reckoned this to be the best place to conceal itself while it waited for the rover to complete the connection procedure, and all the ground operatives to return inside the complex.

Around a half hour later, Gizmo poked its head out, sensing the area now clear of activity. It moved over to one of the vacant docking airlocks, jacked into an exterior data port, and began scanning the internal security feeds.

Even though its primary objective was to deliver the data to the MLOD, now that it had returned to the enclave, new decision forks became apparent. One of which would depend on whether Jann and Nills were still alive. But as it sifted through the enclave's real-time datastream, it could not find any indication of their whereabouts, nor their state of health. Yet, it knew that there were many areas inside the enclave where it had no access, so it was still a possibility that they were viable lifeforms. It considered the option of sneaking in and trying to locate them, and potentially instigating a rescue. But this was an option fraught with a myriad of probabilities, most of which were on the wrong side of optimal. In the end, Gizmo dismissed the option by virtue of it having an extremely low chance of success. Instead, it turned its attention to securing suitable transport so it could execute its primary directive.

There were three rovers currently docked, any of which Gizmo could potentially steal. But they were all old and ran on methane, meaning their range was limited. Still, all it needed was one with enough fuel to get to the waystation. But as Gizmo's silicon brain crunched the numbers, it arrived at an extremely low probability of pulling this off.

First, there was the possibility that it would not get away unnoticed, and the same scenario that had just happened to it may very well play out again. The last time it had been lucky to escape unscathed—other than a broken antenna. This time it might not be so lucky. Secondly, even if it did manage to get to the waystation, there was still a high probability that the Xenonists there would be alerted and be waiting, ready to destroy it at the first opportunity. But Gizmo had another option, one with a far higher probability of success, one where the numbers stacked up.

It was still jacked into the data port, so it scanned the external camera feeds and found the location of the shuttle it had observed landing some time ago. It was parked on a small landing pad on the far side of the enclave. There were no other ships, at least none that the droid could find with a quick scan. This meant that if it could somehow commandeer this ship, then there was a very high probability it would not be followed. And it could get all the way to Jezero City, bypassing the waystation.

It disconnected from the data port and began working its way around the perimeter of the complex. Since it knew the exact location of all the external cameras and motion sensors, Gizmo avoided them with ease. As it came around to the rear of the primary dome, it sensed the wide expanse of the shuttle port concourse spread out ahead, and in the center sat a squat transport ship.

Even though dawn was still a few hours hence and the area was consumed by darkness, this posed little trouble for Gizmo's sensors. It slowly scanned the concourse and found no humans operating outside—the way was clear. Yet by crossing over to the ship, the droid would be exposing itself to both motion detection and a multitude of external camera feeds. But it had no other option. It calculated there was no point in trying to hide or dodge; it would be better to just go for it.

Gizmo broke cover and raced across the concourse as fast as its tracked wheels would allow, leaving a trail of fine dust in its wake. It reached the rear loading door of the craft just as it sensed an airlock door opening in the side of the main facility. Two humans in full EVA suits emerged and started running toward the droid.

Gizmo estimated their distance and speed and

calculated it had three point two seconds before it was in range of their weapons. It jacked into the external loading bay data port and immediately began lowering the rear ramp. But time was of the essence, so it didn't wait for the ramp to fully open. Instead it reached up, extending its right arm, grabbed the lip, and pulled itself up and into the shuttle cargo hold. The droid took a micro-second to reorient itself and locate the internal ramp control panel. It raced over and flipped the lever to close it. As the ramp began to rise up again, Gizmo sensed a human hand grab the lip of the ramp, but let go again as the door finally shut.

The droid spun around and raced for the flight deck. It had only narrowly avoided direct confrontation, and there were still plenty of ways they could prevent it from lifting off. It needed to hurry.

It jacked into the control interface in the flight deck and activated the shuttle's systems. The cockpit lit up like a pinball machine, monitors flickered to life, and the ship rumbled as the engines powered up.

It could now sense several more humans converging on the craft via the ship's external camera feeds. One hefted a high-powered plasma weapon onto his shoulder just as the ship lifted off from the pad. It rose vertically for a few seconds before a blast streaked past the hull, just forward of the right-hand side engine.

The power flickered and flight control went dead for a micro-second before Gizmo coaxed it back to life. The craft bucked and shook as Gizmo applied full power to the lift engines. The ship rose up at speed, spinning around as it did to face in the direction of Jezero City. Gizmo now redirected all power to the main engine, and the craft accelerated away across the barren Plains of Utopia.

20

A FRIEND IN NEED

Mia awoke to the ping of an alert for the entrance door of her accommodation module in the MLOD HQ in Jezero. She glanced at the clock. 4:47 am. *Who the hell is calling at this time?* she thought as she sat up and rubbed a hand over her face. With a tired sigh, she reached over and tapped an icon on the monitor on her bedside locker, activating the front door camera feed.

It was a service droid. *A delivery? At this time?* Mia was about to switch off the monitor and go back to sleep when something triggered in her memory. She wasn't sure what it was exactly, but there was something familiar about this droid. She considered it for a moment, as much as her tired brain would allow, then tapped the intercom. "Go away. It's the middle of the night."

"Mia, it is I, Gizmo."

Mia sat bolt upright and studied the image on the

monitor more closely this time. The droid turned to face the camera and waved.

"Oh my god, Gizmo. What—? How—?" But there were too many questions running through her sleep-fogged brain, each one stumbling over the other as they tried to become vocalized. She gave up, hit the entry button, and rolled out of the bed nook just as Gizmo rolled into her accommodation module.

It looked different than how she remembered it from the last time she saw it at the museum. Apart from the fact that it no longer had a gaping hole in its breastplate, it looked more elegant, more sophisticated.

Gizmo raised an arm. "Greetings, Mia. I see you have suffered some structural damage in my absence."

Mia reflexively glanced at the bandage around her shoulder. "Oh, yeah. It's nothing really, just an argument I got into with some Xenonists."

"I too have had my own troubles with these people."

Mia raised an eyebrow, then gave the droid a considered look. "You'd better tell me all. But first I really need a coffee."

FOR THE NEXT TEN MINUTES, Mia stood dumbfounded at the small kitchen counter in her accommodation module —sipping strong coffee, trying to wake up—as Gizmo gave her a rundown on how it came to be no longer an exhibit in the science museum, its travels to the Xenonist enclave with Malbec and Langthorp, their discovery of the cloning labs, subsequent capture, and Gizmo's extraordinary escape.

"I brought the shuttle in to land just outside the crater wall, over to the south, and made the rest of the journey under my own power. I assumed the Xenonists would have sent word ahead, and be waiting to ambush me if I landed the craft within Jezero.

"I then entered the city via the manual airlock in the old industrial sector, that way I could pass inside undetected. However, when I attempted to interface with the data layer within the colony comms systems, I discovered that I have been locked out—I cannot send the data.

"Apparently, Langthorp's enthusiasm to reactivate me crossed a few red lines for the colony AI. It considered his activities a high-level security breach, so my access has been invalidated. Worse, I am now a wanted droid within the city. Should I be detected, then I am likely to be incarcerated and deactivated. This would be a suboptimal outcome."

"But how did you find me? How did you get in here? I mean, this is the MLOD HQ," Mia said, as she downed the last of the coffee in her mug.

"The AI does not control everything, just higher-level systems, those deemed critical for life support and security. I was able to access the census database and identify your location. Once I knew that, gaining entry was relatively easy. I simply posed as a service droid. No one thought to check my credentials. I passed through as if I were invisible—just another worker going about its business."

Mia poured herself another shot of brew, trying to kick her mind into gear.

"My apologies for disturbing you at this late hour," it continued. "But you are my only hope, Mia. The only human I can trust in Jezero. You will help?"

"Of course I will, Gizmo. You know that." Mia was taken aback by the droid's question, as if it somehow doubted her loyalty. "We absolutely need to get this data to Tarkin." She paused for a beat. "Look, Gizmo," she said a little sheepishly, "for what it's worth, I didn't really feel good about you ending up in the museum again, you know, after all that happened to you."

"My location in time and space has no meaning for me other than it being a set of temporal coordinates. But I do sense that it has meaning for you."

Mia looked at the droid for a moment. Her brain was still not awake enough to understand what Gizmo had just said to her, other than it seemed okay about how things turned out. So she left it at that.

She picked up her slate and handed it to Gizmo. "Download a sample onto this and I can transmit directly to Poe Tarkin, and Bret Stanton—he's heading up the investigation into these guys. I'll tell them to meet us in the Operations Room, where you can give them the rest of the data. Then we can decide what our next move is."

. . .

LESS THAN FIFTEEN MINUTES LATER, when Mia and Gizmo finally arrived at the Operations Room in MLOD HQ, Tarkin, Stanton, and two other high-ranking agents from the security division were already there—all silhouetted in front of the large wall monitor watching the data-stream from Jann and Nills' search of the Xenonist enclave. They turned to acknowledge her in silence as she entered, pausing to give Gizmo the once-over. But their interest in the droid was only momentary; their primary focus was on the imagery unfolding on screen—the cloning tanks could clearly be seen as Jann's flashlight swept over them.

Capt. Nina Aby, the new head of armed security and a close associate of Mia's, moved over and whispered to her, "The droid has more data, I believe?"

"Two point six terabytes," Gizmo replied matter-of-factly as it moved over to interface with a console.

The group's focus moved back to the wall monitor as the feed became less fuzzy, more detailed. Malbec's voice could now be heard annotating as she moved closer to one of the opaque tanks. *"I can see something suspended inside... The liquid is opaque, slightly fluorescent... It's a body... clearly human...definitely a clone."*

Malbec's monologue continued like this for a while, interspersed with comments from Langthorp, as both moved through the vast cloning farm.

"Holy...goddamn...shit?" Tarkin eventually said, as he looked around at the others with astonishment. "I almost can't believe what I'm seeing," he continued, waving a hand at the screen.

"Believe it," said Mia. "I told you they were bringing in a lot more than a few petri dishes."

"They must have been at this a long time, years probably. You were right, Mia," Stanton said, apologetically.

"Well, it was really Zack that got the ball rolling on my end." She paused a beat. "How is he, by the way?"

"Still in intensive care, as far as I know." Stanton's voice was low and sympathetic.

"I think we've all seen enough. I'll pause it here for the moment." Tarkin gestured at the monitor, and the screen froze on a ghostly image of a cloning tank.

"Our first priority has to be the safe return of Malbec and Langthorp." Tarkin turned around to face the group.

"Let's not forget Xenon. If this"—Stanton gestured at the screen—"is true, then he hasn't been in control of this group for a very long time."

"How do we want to handle this?" said Aby. "Do we go in hard and heavy, close them down completely? And what about their enclave here in Jezero?" She directed her question at Tarkin.

He considered this for a moment. "As I said, our first priority has to be Malbec and Langthorp. It's inconceivable that they could be held hostage. So, we must respond with force if necessary. I don't see that we have any other choice."

"I can have two security transports fully loaded and

ready in thirty minutes," said Aby. "Flight time would be another hour. But I need your okay to instigate that directive."

Tarkin glanced at the others, then nodded to Aby. "Do it. But there's going to be hell to pay politically—and a huge shock to the citizens." Tarkin shook his head. "Just when we're getting over the Great Storm. Now this."

"Is there any way that this...has a simple explanation?" Lieutenant Renton, Aby's second-in-command, gestured at the frozen image of the cloning tank on screen. He seemed transfixed by it, as if his brain could not conceive of such a reality.

"The evidence is clear," Mia replied, giving him a cautious look. "Xenon's group has been infiltrated and radicalized over the last few years, and we've all been blind to it. Granted, we had more pressing issues to deal with, what with the storm and all that."

"Agreed," said Tarkin. "We've given this group way too much leeway simply because they're comprised mainly of original colonists. But I don't think you can argue with the data the droid has brought back from the enclave. Xenon is being held captive, and this...clone, Argon, has taken his place, passing himself off as—let's face it—the president of Mars. That in and of itself is a serious crime." Tarkin was getting himself worked up. His face was flushed and his gestures more animated. "And now they've regressed back to the dark days of the colony... back to human cloning. How they thought they could get away with it, I just don't know."

"Maybe there's more to this? A bigger picture?" Mia said, looking around from one to the other.

"You could be right," said Stanton. "I received some new information earlier on this evening that I think collates with what we've seen on the data feed. It's the DNA analysis from the bodies we found at the site of the ship explosion. It shows that both bodies were identical, and I don't mean they're twins—they're clones."

"When did you get this?" said Mia.

"A few hours ago. The analysis took longer than usual —the lab techs wanted to be sure of their findings. However"—Stanton lowered his voice—"it seems that Dr. Jann Malbec knew, or at least suspected this, shortly before she headed to the enclave. I think she might have been looking for the evidence."

"Well, she sure found it," said Aby.

"This would implicate the Xenonists in the attack on the ship as well," Mia said, matter-of-factly.

"It looks that way." Stanton nodded. "But the question now is, to what purpose? What were they trying to achieve with this act? What's their end-game?"

"Does it matter?" Aby interjected. "We know what they're up to now, and we're going to put a stop to it."

"If you're planning a raid on the clearing house here in Jezero, then I want in," Mia said as she pointed a finger at Stanton.

"Mia, seriously, you don't have to do this," he replied.

"These guys tried to kill me and Zack. They killed an innocent civilian in the process, so as far as I'm concerned, it's payback time. Also, I want to know what they're hiding in there, what's so important that they needed to get rid of anyone snooping around."

"And we're going to find out, Mia," said Stanton. "But you don't need to go putting yourself in harm's way again. You're still not back in action yet. So the answer is no, let us deal with this."

Mia gave him a stern look and folded her arms. Her shoulder chose this exact time to send a bolt of pain through her upper body; she cringed a little. *Goddammit,* she thought, *not now.*

"Look, Mia," said Tarkin, "for what it's worth, you were right. These guys are up to no good, and too much deference has been given to them. We all appreciate the hit you took on this, and Zack too. But your work is done. Leave the mop-up job to us."

Mia considered this for a moment. They were right—she was not physically up to the task, she could get herself killed, and there was no need. So she resigned herself to sitting this one out. "Okay. But there is one thing you can do for me."

"Sure, what is it?" said Tarkin.

"Langthorp did something to upset the primary colony AI when he was reactivating Gizmo here." She jerked a thumb at the droid. "Now it's locked out, and also flagged a security risk. I need it reinstated."

The director slowly nodded as he thought through this request. "Very well. I see no problem with reinstating its security credentials. I'll see to it straightaway."

"And AI access?" Mia pressed.

Tarkin screwed his mouth up. "Hmmm...that's a little trickier. There could be blowback from the Council on that."

"Look, this droid is the only reason we're all sitting around the table. It's the only reason we know what's going on. So, you all owe it."

Tarkin sighed. "Okay, goddammit, Mia. I'll sign off on it. But the droid is now your responsibility. You give me your word that you'll keep it under your control?"

"With pleasure. I would consider it an honor." She turned to Gizmo and gave it the thumbs-up.

Aby pressed a hand to her ear, then looked over at Tarkin. "I've just got word, the shuttles are being readied now, sir."

The director nodded. "Good. Let's put an end to this cloning activity." He turned to Stanton. "Get your people prepared for a raid on the clearing house. I want them all brought in and everything shut down."

21

FAILURE TO COMPLY

Jann awoke to the sound of the lock being thrown on the door to their cell. Three Xenonist guards entered, one of whom gestured at her. "Come with us, Argon wants to talk."

She sat up and glanced over at Nills. He was still asleep, but looking considerably better—the color had returned to his face, the skin around the wound on his chest was healing, and his breathing was easier. Her entreaties to Argon had borne fruit, and a medic had been dispatched to treat him. That was yesterday.

"Okay, wait outside. I'll be there in a minute."

The guards looked unsure.

"Just go," Jann said as she pointed at the door.

Reluctantly, they left the cell.

She quickly threw on her flight-suit and boots and quietly checked on Nills. Xenon, who was lying on the floor nearby, snapped his eyes open and sat up with a jerk.

Jann raised a hand. "It's okay, they're taking me to Argon. He wants to talk. I'll be back."

Xenon relaxed a little.

"Just keep an eye on Nills, okay?"

He nodded. "Will do. Just be careful."

JANN WAS BROUGHT to the viewing chamber, just off the primary biodome. It was the same place where they had been entertained on the first evening—where Argon had been masquerading as Xenon. But now the space had a spartan feel, the clutter had been removed, and all that remained was a semicircle of low seating and a large holo-table. Argon and several other hooded figures stood around this table studying a holographic projection of some sort. Jann didn't recognize it. He turned to her when she entered and beckoned her over. "Ah, Dr. Malbec, there you are. Come, I have something to show you."

Jann cautiously moved over to the holo-table.

"It would appear that droid of yours is made of strong stuff," said Argon, as the image on the table changed to a camera feed. She immediately recognized it as the main thoroughfare in Jezero City—and highlighted in the crowd was a grainy image of Gizmo. Her heart skipped a beat. The little droid had actually made it.

"It has defied all our attempts to eliminate it," Argon continued. "Even managing to give our agents the slip in

Jezero City. Therefore, all that data you so surreptitiously obtained has been handed over to the MLOD."

Jann stepped back from the table and gave Argon a cold, hard look. "Then the game is up, Argon. You can't continue with this any more—you must hand yourself over."

Argon threw his head back and laughed. It seemed a genuine laugh, and irritated her. *How can he be so cavalier, now that the secret is out?* she thought.

"Our houses in Jezero and Syrtis are already being raided. But this was to be expected. They will not find anything, and our plans are unaffected." Argon waved a dismissive hand in the air.

"But they now know where we are. They'll be coming for myself and Nills, and Xenon too," said Jann, trying to reason with him.

"They're already on their way." Argon tapped an icon on the holo-table, and an image appeared of two transport ships hurtling across the surface of Mars. "You see, they come for you."

"Then give it up now. You can't win." Jann sounded exasperated.

"Ah...but this is where you are wrong, Dr. Malbec. You see, this is just the beginning." He tapped another icon, and a camera feed materialized showing a vast room full of Xenonists arming themselves. "Our numbers, as you can see, are considerable. We will not go down easily."

Jann shook her head. "It doesn't matter, Argon. They'll simply reinforce. You can't hope to defeat them."

He went silent for a moment, giving her a long-considered look. "You are correct, of course," he finally said, breaking his stare to look back at the image on the holo-table. "Ultimately we can't defeat them this way, and many will die. But this is why I called you. This is where you can help."

"Help you? And why would I do that?"

"Because that was the deal, remember?" He jerked a finger at her.

Jann didn't reply.

"However, I'm also confident that once you know our true intentions, you will understand that storming our enclave is a futile exercise for the MLOD forces. One in which many of our people will needlessly die. This can all be averted if you persuade them that you are safe and well, and are here to support our cause. Also, that you were mistaken in your assessment of the bio-labs. They are, in fact, for food production, not cloning."

Jann's gut reaction was to tell him to go screw himself. But she decided to buy some time instead. "What...intentions?"

He lowered his head as if considering something, then gave her a sideways look. "You and I are cut from the same cloth, Dr. Malbec."

"I beg to differ. There's nothing we have in common."

Argon ignored her. "Do you remember your very first days on Mars, your first arrival at the colony?"

Jann just gave a shrug.

"Of course you do—they are what define you. A

colony ravaged by a pathogen that altered your DNA. So you age slow and heal fast, just like all those original colonists from that time."

"Those lucky enough to have survived," said Jann.

"True, but you were made stronger, enhanced, elevated one more notch up on the evolutionary tree—a superior human."

Jann remained silent. *Let him rant*, she thought.

"Those first biological seeds were then expanded upon and brought to new heights by the great Dr. Vanji. Langthorp is a product of his genius. But his finest moment was the creation of Xenon Hybrid. The first true evolution in the Homo sapiens line. Yet, Xenon would go on to waste this power, this purity, on wandering and philosophical ramblings.

"While all the time the pioneers, the originals, were being pushed aside by the Earth-based corporations exploiting the planet for its wealth. Look around you, Malbec—what do you see? Syrtis is an industrial hellhole and Jezero a playground for the wealthy tourist. Is this what we are? Is this what we have become?"

"It is what it is," was all Jann could manage by way of a reply.

"Well, that's about to change. A new dawn is beginning on Mars, one that will shine on the true inheritors of this planet. Those who will forge a new and great society. We will build a home for a superior race, a higher order of human."

"I've heard all this before, Argon—a long time ago, and it didn't end well then, either."

"By your hand, Jann Malbec. Yours and Langthorp. But Vanji was a fool, even if he was a genius. He was lured by the offer of a temple built to accommodate his ego. Do not fear, I have no such illusions. What we are building here is nothing short of a new civilization."

"Why are you telling me all this?"

"Because of who you are. I assumed that you of all people would understand. Unlike Xenon, who cannot bring himself to accept what needs to be done. He was the one who showed us the way, he shone a light upon the path, but he himself would not, nor could not, take it. For a long time, those of us from original stock, the early colonists and those who were a product of Dr. Vanji's genius—that includes Langthorp and Xenon—have suffered the ignominy of having our planet, our home, cannibalized by interlopers whose only objective is the exploitation of its resources for the benefit of Earth.

"You have sensed this disillusionment, Malbec. I know you have. Some of us sought solace in Xenon and his vision, and we migrated here to this enclave and built a place for ourselves. But over time it became clear to many of us that we were a dying breed, at risk of being consigned to the history books. Our planet was being taken from us, and if we did not do something more radical, then we would be nothing more than a curiosity. The problem was that there were too few of us, so an idea began to take shape to use the greed of the Earth-based corporation for our own ends. We would offer a select cohort the prospect of reestablishing human genetic engineering. Of course, their greed made them jump at the chance. And soon we began to implement Dr. Vanji's process. But we have refined that. This way we could multiply the people and resources to enact the next phase, which is where we're now at."

"Next phase?"

"Sir, the MLOD shuttles have landed and are deploying troops."

The image on the holo-table shifted to an external camera feed. Jann could see the rear ramps of the craft lowering and groups of well-armed MLOD security personnel being deployed, fanning out across the landing pad.

"They're contacting us, sir."

"Put it up on screen."

A 3D head-and-shoulders image of an MLOD captain blossomed above the holo-table. "This is Captain Nina Aby. We have reason to believe you are holding Dr. Jann Malbec, Nills Langthorp, and Xenon Hybrid against their will and that you are conducting illicit cloning operations within this facility. You are required to hand them over and allow us free and unrestricted access to your facility. Failure to comply will result in forced entry and unnecessary violence. I'm sure you would wish to avoid that. You have one hour."

"And so it begins." Argon extinguished the comms connection, and the image flickered off. He turned to

Jann. "Now it's time for you to record your message." He leaned in close to her. "And make sure it's persuasive."

Jann glared at him for a moment. "Go screw yourself."

Argon sighed. "I see. Well, I'm disappointed. Let me remind you that failure to comply will render your existence, and Langthorp's, somewhat pointless. You will both be recycled."

Jann held his gaze for a moment. "You need to end this, Argon. You need to let us go. You must realize this is a fight you can't win."

He stepped back and seemed to be considering something. "You see, that's where you're wrong, Dr. Malbec." He turned his back to her and gazed out across the barren Martian surface. "I believe your last question, before we were interrupted, was concerning the next phase. So, let me explain the reality to you. It was a humble bacterium that altered your DNA, Dr. Malbec, back in the early days of the colony. And we considered that a similar bacterium might provide us with an elegant solution to our problem. Therefore, we engineered a pathogen, fatal to all those infected whose DNA does not match a specific profile. In other words, it will eradicate all human life from the face of Mars that has no right to be here."

Jann felt as if the ground had just opened up underneath her and she was now entering a parallel universe, a sinister dimension where all humanity and morality held no sway. "You're not seriously considering the mass murder of thousands of innocent people?"

"This is a purge, a cleansing. There is no room for sentimentality."

"You need to stop this now. You need to think about what you're doing."

"It's too late, it's already in progress. Granted, your droid alerting the MLOD in Jezero City meant we needed to amend our plans. But soon, a pathogen will be released into the internal atmosphere in Jezero. It has a three-sol incubation period, so will have time to travel to all points of human population on Mars. From Jezero to Syrtis to Elysium, to the research stations and outposts. It is fatal to all who are not purebred, there is no escape, and no human from Earth will be able to set foot on Mars again. In this way, we will reclaim the planet."

"You have lost your goddamn mind, Argon," Jann almost shouted.

"Hmmm...I now see that I was naive in my thinking you could be enlightened. You are like Xenon, visionary only to the point where hard decisions need to be made." He waved a hand in the air. "Our conversation is over. You will be returned to your accommodation while I decide when you are to be recycled." He turned and gave her a cold, hard look. "Then again, maybe it would be better for you to live and witness this new world we are creating. You will, of course, not be affected by the pathogen. You are one of us, after all. Whether you like it or not."

22

NETWORK NODE

When Jann returned to the room that constituted their prison cell, her sense of foreboding and helplessness was mitigated by the sight of Nills. He was now upright and alert.

"Nills...you're back," she exclaimed, and rushed to embrace him.

"Ow...easy." He gave her a grin as they disentangled. "So, what did Argon want?" His face turned serious.

Jann wasted no time in relaying all that Argon had revealed to her, his manic plans, and his demands that she help him.

"That's...insane," Nills said as he paced around the room. It seemed as if he had built up a reserve of energy while unconscious, and now that he had been rejuvenated, he needed to expend it somehow.

"It comes as no surprise to me that this is the end

game," Xenon offered. He sat cross-legged on a low bed and was the picture of calm, in total contrast to Nills.

"For a long time, I wondered why they were creating so many clones," he said. "All they needed to satisfy the Earth-based corporation that was funding this was one or two as proof of concept. Then they could have taken this proven technology back to Earth. But I could see that Argon and his followers were creating dozens of full-grown humans. I had struggled to understand why—now I know. All to create this new, enhanced civilization on Mars."

"We have to stop him," said Nills. "Whatever it takes."

"How?" Jann sounded genuinely desperate. "We're locked up tight in here, and even if we could get out, what can we do against an army of fanatics?"

Nills stopped his pacing. "Getting out is not a problem."

Jann looked at him with a certain skepticism. "Really?"

"Yes, I had a look at the lock. Old-school tech, easy to bypass, shouldn't be a problem."

"And then what?" said Jann, skeptically.

"We need a way to contact Jezero, warn them of what's about to happen," Xenon said as he unfolded himself and stood up. Jann could sense he was beginning to get his mojo back.

"Contacting Jezero could be tricky." Nills started pacing again, then suddenly stopped. "You said the MLOD captain contacted the enclave?"

"Yes," said Jann. "Just a one-way holo-message, an ultimatum. But Argon gave no reply."

"Doesn't matter, there will be a log of it." Nills paused for a moment as if considering something. "Apart from the bio-labs," he continued, "the tech here is archaic. They don't have an AI, they don't even use droids, and the comms setup is very...rudimentary." He stopped pacing and looked from one to the other. "They use a network of nodes throughout the facility that connects all personnel services. Those nodes then transmit back to a base station that manages the traffic. All we need to do is find one of those nodes, and we have a good chance of establishing a comms connection. It may even be possible to trace the log file for the captain's message, and we'll have a way to contact her directly."

"So where do we find one of these...nodes?" Jann still wasn't convinced.

"I know where they are," said Xenon. "There's one close by, in the control room for the main bio-lab. It's not far from here, on the same level as this."

"Okay," Jann finally said after a beat. "It's as good a plan as any. I have no idea when they're going to release the pathogen, but it's soon. So, time is critical."

"Then let's go." Nills moved over to the entrance door and started taking apart the control panel with a tool he had fashioned from a small scrap of metal. This was followed by a period of prodding and poking, and a moment of head-scratching, before they heard the locking bolt thump open. Nills stood back from the panel with a wide grin on his face. "Okay Xenon, lead the way. Let's find that communication node."

THE MAIN CLONING cavern was still dark when they entered, with just the faint greenish glow from the tanks to illuminate their path. Xenon went ahead and seemed familiar with the route he was taking them. Jann listened intently for any sound that might indicate the presence of other people. But it was eerily quiet, except for the gentle background hum of machines and the gurgle of some pump or other.

Nills also noticed the silence. "Where is everybody?" he whispered. "I was expecting there to be some workers here?"

"They've probably been redeployed to the main facility entry points, preparing to repel the assault from the MLOD," Jann replied, in an equally hushed tone.

By now, Xenon had shepherded them across the center of the cavern, then he halted and pointed ahead. "That's the control room."

Jann poked her head out from behind a tank and could see a window that ran along the far wall for around five meters. Through it could be seen an area populated with workstations and equipment. It was dimly lit, and Jann could only make out one person.

"I see someone moving around in there. But there may be more. How do we want to do this?" She turned back to the others.

"Leave it to me," Xenon said as he raised his hood over his head and boldly walked toward the access doorway.

"What's he doing?" said Nills, a little concerned.

Jann didn't reply. Instead, they both watched from behind the shelter of a cloning tank as Xenon casually strolled into the control room and seemed to strike up a conversation with the tech working in there.

"They think he's Argon," Jann whispered.

"Of course," said Nills. "I keep forgetting they're both identical."

Another tech came out from the depths of the room and joined the first one.

"There's two of them," he whispered.

Suddenly, Xenon struck one of them in the throat, and he dropped to the floor clutching his neck. The second tech was so shocked he didn't have time to respond before he too was struck down. For a moment, Xenon stood over the collapsed figures, then hunkered down out of sight.

"What's he doing?"

Nills's question was answered when Xenon stood up again holding two plasma pistols. He moved over to the window and motioned to them to come in. Jann and Nills both broke cover and dashed across the tank room.

"Here, take these," Xenon said as they entered. "I don't want them." He handed Jann the weapons, then gestured at the fallen bodies. "Help me tie these guys up, before they regain consciousness."

Jann helped Xenon bind and gag the two hapless techs while Nills scoured the area, looking for the communications node. He found it exactly where Xenon said it would be, located in an innocuous stack of servers sectioned off in two locked cabinets with transparent doors. He jimmied one of the doors open and slid out a metal drawer revealing a headset, an interface, and a basic 2D screen that popped up when the drawer was fully extended. Jann and Xenon joined him when they had finished with the techs.

"Will it work?" Jann leaned in to look at the setup.

"Give me a minute." Nills booted up the interface, and the screen filled with data schematics. "Good, good," he muttered to himself. "This just might work," he said again as his fingers danced over the interface. The data on screen seemed to explode into a myriad of icons and options.

"You hear that?" Xenon cocked his head slightly, straining to listen. "A voice, someone calling."

They froze, remained very still for a beat, and sure enough Jann could hear it, coming from the entrance to the control room.

She whispered to Nills. "You keep working, we'll go deal with this." She looked at Xenon, who nodded back.

Nills reached into his belt, pulled out the plasma pistol, and offered it to Xenon. "Here, you might need this."

"No." He raised a palm. "I think I can manage without one."

"Just set it to stun if you don't want to kill anyone," Nills suggested.

"I know, but I prefer to take a more subtle approach."

Nills nodded and shoved the pistol back in his belt.

Jann, however, had no such qualms. She pulled out the weapon, checked it was ready for action, and held it concealed behind her back. Xenon led the way, striding forward as if he owned the place. Which, in a way, he did.

They met a well-armed Xenonist guard face on, just inside the entrance door. He'd been calling out for one of the techs, but when he saw Xenon, he stopped dead in his tracks with a look of both awe and confusion.

"Eh, I'm very sorry to have bothered you, Master Argon. I didn't realize you were here," he said, with visible deference.

"That's okay," Xenon said in a smooth, calming tone as he strode forward, coming up close to the guard before striking him in the throat with the side of his hand. He dropped like a wet towel.

"You must teach me that some time, Xenon," said Jann.

"With pleasure." He knelt beside the fallen guard and started relieving him of his weapons. They tied him up and stashed him in the same storage room with the others. By the time Jann got back to Nills, he was deep into studying lines of code.

"Any joy?" she said as she approached.

Nills pointed at the screen. "Found it. That's the log entry for Capt. Aby's comm. I think we're ready to give this a try." He glanced up at her. "Any trouble back there?"

"Nothing Xenon couldn't handle with his throat chop. But I think that guard was looking for the one of the techs, so there could be more soon if they can't contact any."

Nills slotted in an earpiece and tapped an icon on the interface. "Here goes." He raised a thumb to Jann. "Captain Aby, this is Nills Langthorp. Are you receiving me?"

There was a pause before Nills jerked his head to look at Jann and give her the thumbs-up.

"Yes... We're still alive. Yes, Malbec and Xenon. Hold on... I'm handing you over to Dr. Malbec now." He removed the earpiece and handed it to her. "It's best you speak to her, but be quick."

She slotted it into her ear. "Aby?"

"Dr. Malbec, good to hear your voice. You had us worried. Can you give me an update on the situation in there?"

"There's probably over a hundred well-armed Xenonists here, just ready and waiting for you to stage an assault on the facility. You're totally outnumbered."

"I see, appreciate the intel. Any way for you to get out?"

"Negative. But that's a minor issue now, because there's a more sinister threat coming. You need to listen to me very carefully, because we don't have much time. They're planning to release a pathogen in Jezero City. It's fatal to all but those with altered DNA. Only the original colonists, and the Xenonists, are immune."

"Holy shit, that's like ninety percent of the population."

"Yes, it's insane. They want to return Mars to the founders, or some such bullshit. You need to get this to MLOD HQ right now, maybe they have a chance to find it."

"Do you know where or when?"

"No, all I know is it's airborne and it's soon."

"Okay, relaying your message now. Can you stay connected?"

"No, we're exposed here, got to move. We may get another chance later. Forget about us—and don't try to storm the facility, just concentrate on finding that pathogen site."

"Acknowledged."

Jann took out the earpiece and handed it back to Nills. "Well, we've done all we can. Now it's in the lap of the gods."

23

ATMOSPHERE PROCESSING

With the MLOD HQ in Jezero beginning to fill up with people arrested during the raid on the clearing house, Stanton decided it was time for Mia to vacate and return to the hotel. The threat to her life had passed, and HQ was going to get very busy processing and interrogating the influx of Xenonists. There was nothing more for her, or Gizmo, to do here. They would just be getting in the way.

Mia considered objecting, seeing as how there was still no word back from the enclave, no update on whether Jann and Nills were still alive. But Stanton assured her that he would keep her informed. So Mia packed up her bag, and with Gizmo in tow, headed back to the hotel.

. . .

THE FRONT FACADE had been repaired, leaving nothing to indicate that a shoot-out had occurred here only a few sols ago. Seeing it brought Zack back into her mind. *I should really go and see him again*, she thought. *See how he's doing.* She heard that he was out of danger now, so that was something, at least. Yet she was not sure if he was conscious or still in an induced coma. Mia decided to get settled back into the hotel first, and then she would visit him.

"Ah...Envoy Sorelli, you have returned." A sleek lobby droid shuffled up in front of her. "I see you have brought your own droid with you. Does this mean that you are dissatisfied with the standard of droid provided by our humble establishment?"

"No, it's a long story. Now if you don't mind..." Mia dodged the lobby droid and headed for the elevator.

"If I may," the droid call after her. "Unfortunately, I must inform you that your suite is no longer available."

Mia stopped, turned around, and stared at it for second. "Well, just give me a different one."

"Again, I regret to inform you that this will not be possible."

Mia moved a few paces to face it. "Why the hell not?"

"A small matter of an outstanding bill...for damages."

"What? Not my problem, buddy." She poked an angry finger at it. "Take it up with your insurance or the MLOD."

"We have, but I am afraid the situation remains unresolved."

"Perhaps I could be of assistance," Gizmo said as it approached the lobby droid.

"I fail to see how. Unless you can regularize the account." The lobby droid gave Gizmo a cursory scan.

"I am certain your request can be accommodated," Gizmo replied. "But first it would be prudent for me to satisfy Envoy Sorelli that the accounting is above board. Not that I imagine this establishment would stoop to any unsavory practices."

"I assure you, you will find our standards to be impeccable. Please feel free to interface with our systems so you can be satisfied with our fiduciary credentials."

"Thank you, I am sure it is all in order, as you say."

The lobby droid led Gizmo over to its dock, a sort of lobby desk, behind which the main interface for the hotel AI was located. Gizmo jacked in. Mia watched from the sidelines as Gizmo analyzed the data. A moment later it disengaged.

"Please correct me if I am wrong, but it seems to me that the bill has been rescinded, and that Envoy Sorelli has free access to all hotel services—for life."

The lobby droid twitched a little, then it too jacked in. "That is very curious. But you are quite correct. I do not understand how I was not informed of this change in status." It disengaged and turned to Mia. "My sincerest apologies for this terrible mix-up. I was not aware of the latest data update. Please, allow me to show you to our best suite, personally."

Mia raised a hand. "That's okay, not a problem. These

things happen. If you don't mind, we'll see ourselves to the suite. I know where it is."

"Certainly, by all means. And please do not hesitate to let me know if there is anything, and I mean anything, you require to make your stay with us more pleasurable."

"Okay, Gizmo, let's go." She jerked her head in the direction of the elevator. Once inside, Mia burst out laughing as soon as the doors closed. "Gizmo, you're a class act. Glad to have you watching my back again."

"My pleasure, I am here to help."

The elevator rose up and opened directly into the penthouse suite. "Nice." Mia looked around the wide expanse of the room, tastefully furnished in sleek, minimalist-designed furnishing, with accents of old-Earth rustic charm. She threw her bag down on one of the long, low sofas and made her way to a well-stocked bar.

"I could sure use a stiff drink," Mia said as she poured herself a bourbon on the rocks. She took a sip and expelled a satisfying sigh as she sat on one of the well-upholstered bar stools. "You know, Gizmo, I might never leave here, now that I am a VIP guest—for life."

"I am sorry to inform you that there are only twenty-eight sols to the next accounting period. After that, questions will be asked and the number of those inquiries will only rise exponentially thereafter."

"Okay, so I've only got twenty-eight sols. That's still good." Mia took another sip of bourbon and stepped down from the bar stool, intending to explore the rest of the suite.

"Incoming call," Gizmo announced. "From Bret Stanton."

Mia looked at the droid, a little confused.

"I took the liberty of monitoring your comms channel. I thought it might be helpful."

"Eh, sure, no problem. Better connect me, then."

"I will put it on the main screen."

A section of one wall flickered into life, and the head and shoulders of Bret Stanton materialized. "Mia, we have a major problem."

"What? What problem?"

"First, some good news. We've just been contacted by Dr. Jann Malbec. She's still inside the enclave, but she's alive and well, and so are Langthorp and Xenon."

"Well that's good. Can they get them out?"

"No, not yet. Too many armed Xenonists. But that's not a priority now. Malbec has informed us that the Xenonists are planning to—and you're probably not going to believe this —release a deadly airborne pathogen somewhere in Jezero."

Mia almost dropped her glass. "Holy shit," she said as she gently sat down on a sofa. "That's crazy, why would they do that?"

"They have immunity, apparently. So do all the original colonists, the pioneers. The problem is that all the rest of us don't. That's thousands of citizens."

"Are you saying they want to exterminate us?"

"Insane as it sounds, that seems to be the plan. So we urgently need to find the release site and stop it—and we don't have much time. We found nothing at the clearing house, but we're doing another search. It's all hands on deck, so if you have any ideas, anything that cropped up in your investigation, tell me now."

Mia shook her head. "No, nothing. The clearing house is the only place I can think of."

Bret gave a sigh. "Okay, well it was worth a shot. I gotta go, everybody's being drafted into the search."

The connection terminated.

Mia sat for a moment and tried to mentally digest this revelation. An airborne pathogen. Crazy. Insane. She downed the bourbon in one gulp. *Why would they do something like that?* she wondered. But the *why* was not important. Finding it was what mattered now.

She reached into her bag, pulled out her slate, and navigated to where she had stored the encrypted manifest files. "Gizmo?"

"Yes, Mia."

"There's something I was working on, maybe it's not important anymore, but I was investigating the makeup of all the shipments to the Xenonists since before the Great Storm." She handed the slate to Gizmo. "I only got so far and I ran into a problem—some of the files after the storm are encrypted. I can't get into them, and nobody in the department has authorization to access them."

Gizmo took the slate and interfaced with it. "So you want me to hack them for you."

"Is that possible?"

"Now that I am reconnected to the colony AI, I should be able to utilize its processing power to speed up the decryption task." It raised a metal finger in the air. "Just give me a moment."

Mia went to pour herself another stiff one as Gizmo went to work.

"Done," it said after a few seconds, and handed the slate back to Mia.

She took it and glanced at the screen. All the files were now accessible, but there were hundreds, possibly thousands of line items. "Thanks, Gizmo. It's going to take me some time to work through all these—and we don't have time."

"Perhaps I could rationalize the data for you?"

"Rationalize?"

"Yes, organize it into a more meaningful overview."

"You can do that?"

Gizmo didn't answer. Instead, it proffered a hand to take Mia's slate. A few moments later, Gizmo handed it back. "Here you go. My apologies for the crudity of the presentation, but it is a first pass through all the files."

Mia studied the screen. "Wow, that's incredible."

"My pleasure," replied the droid.

The information was presented in searchable, cross-indexed lists. Product inventory was arranged by type, quantity, port of entry, port of origin, destination, time of sol, and more. Mia scrolled down and paused over a list of final destinations.

Most of the supplies and equipment coming in ended up going to the enclave—others to the clearing house in Jezero and to Syrtis. But there was one other destination on the list that Mia had not seen before, and it seemed to be taking in a significant quantity of inventory. She flipped the slate around to show it to Gizmo and pointed at the location address. "Any idea where this is?"

Gizmo scanned the location data, then activated a map of Jezero City on the main wall monitor. "It is here." A blinking icon identified the exact location.

Mia moved over and studied the map. "That's way over in the industrial sector, very near the atmosphere processing plant. Strange location. I wonder what they were doing all the way over there?"

"Perhaps they wished for cleaner air? My analysis shows a slightly lower particulate count in that sector."

"Air, shit! That could be the release site. We'd better get this to Bret. Can you connect me, Gizmo?"

A few seconds later, a very harassed-looking Bret Stanton appeared on the wall screen. He was outside a building that Mia didn't recognize with a considerable number of MLOD agents. "What is it, Mia?"

"I may have a lead, a location that cropped up from those shipment manifests. It's beside the main atmosphere processor for the old industrial sector."

But Mia could sense from Stanton's demeanor that he

wasn't interested. "We've got a lead here, Mia. One of the Xenonists talked. It wasn't pretty, but he talked."

"How do you know he's not bullshitting you, Bret? Did you beat it out of him? They'll say anything to make it stop."

"It's what we got, so we're following up. I'll try and get someone to check your lead as soon as I can. Sorry, but I gotta go."

The transmission ended.

Mia was silent for a moment as her focus returned to the location of the atmosphere processing plant displayed on her slate. "Gizmo, I don't think we can just wait here and hope that Bret gets his act together to send a team over there."

She put down the slate, reached into her bag again, and this time pulled out her pistol. She checked it for charge, stood up, and shoved it into her jacket pocket.

"You mean we are embarking on another adventure?"

Mia looked over at the droid. "Yup. Just like old times, eh, Gizmo?"

"Indeed. Hopefully I will not be incinerated this time."

24

TIME TO GET REAL

"We can't stay here. We need to find a place to lie low, keep out of sight." Jann turned to Xenon. "Any suggestions, since you know this facility intimately?"

Xenon thought for a moment. "The bulk of the brethren will be guarding the perimeter airlocks, and they're all at surface level. So the best place to hide out would be down in the subterranean levels."

"Okay, let's get going," Nills said as he checked his plasma weapon.

"No, not for me. I am done hiding," Xenon announced.

"But we can't hang around here," Jann pleaded. "For all we know there's a cohort of Xenonists heading our way right now."

"There may well be, and I don't intend to stay here either. I'm going to find Argon and I'm going to kill him."

"Are you nuts, Xenon? You'll never get to him without being taken down, it would be suicide," Nills added to Jann's plea for rationality.

"Be that as it may," Xenon replied. "But this is my intention. For too long I've stood by while Argon and his followers corrupted my life's work. I chose instead the path of nonconfrontation, hoping he would change his ways. But alas, by the time I realized my mistake, it was too late, the damage had been done. Now, all I have achieved is to allow a great evil to spawn in my name. No more. I will take my vengeance this sol or I will die in the attempt."

Jann looked over at Nills, who stood open-mouthed and mute, his mind having trouble processing Xenon's sudden desire for retribution.

"That may be noble, Xenon. But you'll just be throwing your life away," Nills finally said, trying to dissuade his old friend from such a reckless course of action.

"So how do you propose to 'right this wrong?' Just walk right on up and strangle him?" Jann tried to present the absurdity of his line of thinking.

"I know you both think I'm being totally irrational. But it's not as crazy as it sounds. You need to consider that he will not be expecting it. All his people are defending the perimeter airlocks, he will be unguarded. I might never get this opportunity again."

There was a moment's silence as they contemplated this. Jann glanced over at Nills to judge his reaction. She could tell that he was also thinking what she was thinking. That maybe Xenon was right, this wasn't such a crazy idea after all.

"Let me show you," Xenon said as he moved over to a holo-table in the control room and brought up a 3D schematic of the enclave. "Argon is probably here, in the viewing chamber just off the primary dome. That's where he feels safe." Xenon pointed to the sector on a wireframe schematic.

"He will have some of the main hierarchy with him, but everyone else will be gathered around these perimeter airlocks." The projection rotated and zoomed out to show all the subterranean levels. "We are all the way down here." He pointed at a location on one of the lower levels. "I can move up through this central elevator here. It's less likely to be used by the fighters defending the primary enclave access points."

Jann stood back and considered this. "What about cameras?"

"Yes, that may be a problem," Xenon conceded.

"Not if we disguise ourselves as followers," Jann said, jerking a thumb at the storage room.

"Are you planning to go along with this, Jann?" Nills looked troubled.

"If there's a chance we can corner Argon, then there's a chance we can find out the location of the release site— even if we have to beat it out of him."

Nills nodded. "Maybe." But he returned his focus to the 3D schematic, studying it closely without saying anything. He pointed at a long, narrow tunnel that extended way beyond the main structure. "What's that?"

Xenon leaned in. "That's a service tunnel. It goes all the way to an old power station." He rotated the projection and zoomed out. "Over there, around a kilometer away. It used to house a small nuclear power plant, back in the early days when this was a research station. It was decommissioned a long time ago when they retrofitted a fusion reactor."

Jann pointed at where this service tunnel connected with the facility. "It looks like access to that tunnel is on the same level as us, not too far from here."

"Are you thinking of using it as a way out?" said Nills.

"No, I'm thinking it may be a way for Capt. Aby's squad to get in." She turned to Xenon. "We could check it out on our way, see how well guarded it is."

Xenon considered this. "All the main airlocks are at ground level, and that's where I assume Argon will have most of his fighters. This service tunnel is subterranean, so it's possible there are only a few people guarding it. If we take this route through here, then we may be able to get an idea of the numbers." Xenon stood back. "But this does not change my mind. I'm going for Argon. Nothing is going to stop me from that task."

"Is there another comms node in that sector, near the access tunnel?" said Nills.

"Yes, there's several in the vicinity." Xenon tapped an icon on the holo-table, and a series of markers flashed up on the schematic showing the communication network arrangement.

"We need to go, we're running out of time," Jann finally said.

BEFORE LEAVING THE CONTROL ROOM, Jann relieved the tied-up Xenonists of their cloaks. It wouldn't pass close inspection, but should be enough to fool the security cameras. She checked her weapons and shoved two flash grenades she had found on one of the guards into a pocket. "Okay, let's get moving."

Xenon's intimate knowledge of the complex allowed them to minimize the possibility of being detected. But Xenon pushed this to the limit, moving at a blistering pace, so much so that both Jann and Nills had to sprint to keep up. It was a speed that Jann regarded as reckless. They could literally run into to a group of Xenonists around any corner, and that would end all chance they had of reaching Argon.

But their luck held, and Xenon finally came to an abrupt halt at the entrance to a large cavern. He pressed his back against the side wall, signaling to Jann and Nills to do the same. He pointed ahead. "The access door for the service tunnel is around two hundred meters, on the left," he whispered, then began to slowly inch forward.

The cavern was well illuminated and looked like a junkyard for redundant electrical equipment. Along the side wall on the left, a great mountain of this junk had been piled up in front of the service tunnel airlock. The Xenonists were clearly aware that this could be a potential incursion point. But aside from the physical barricade, there were only around six guards that they could see. All grouped behind the cover of some hastily assembled junk, where they had mounted a small plasma cannon. Other than that, their weapons looked basic.

"What do you think?" Jann whispered to Nills.

"Let's call it in, and Capt. Aby can decide if it's worth it."

Xenon jerked his head back the way they came. "This way, follow me."

He brought them back down the passageway around one hundred meters and stopped in front of a dilapidated steel door, recessed into the side wall. A crude sign was stenciled on it, reading, *Network Node C17*.

Jann and Nills took out their pistols as Xenon slowly turned the handle and opened it. The room was small, with racks of equipment crammed along all four walls. There was no illumination save for the glow of a myriad of blinking lights from the servers. Other than that, it was empty.

Nills took out a flashlight and scanned the racks, looking for a comms unit. "Got it," he whispered as he cracked open the door of the unit and went to work.

25

DESERTED

An autonomous ground car brought Mia and Gizmo through the central city district, still busy with people going about their business, oblivious to the impending crisis that was unfolding. From there, the car headed west into the food production sector with its vast hydroponic agri-domes and distribution warehouses. This eventually gave way to a light manufacturing sector and finally onto the atmosphere processing area. Here, the car would go no farther. From this point on they would have to travel on foot.

They disembarked at a large, almost circular airlock system that generally demarcated each sector of the city. These were internal and designed to cordon off an area in an emergency if any loss of pressure was detected.

The car promptly moved off, back into the central city in accordance with whatever parameters were programmed into its algorithm. Mia glanced around at the tall industrial infrastructure all around them. "This place looks like it's seen better days. I hope it's safe."

Gizmo led the way because its internal map knew the route. "This way. It's not far. Approximately a half kilometer past this sector's gateway."

The entire area seemed to be deserted, and they didn't meet a single person as they navigated their way through the maze. A few droids passed by, but paid them no notice.

The atmosphere processing plant was in fact a multitude of units scattered over a relatively large area. It sucked in vast quantities of the thin Martian air and broke it down into its constituent parts. This mostly consisted of CO_2 from which the oxygen was extracted in a bioreactor. This ended up being the oxygen that the citizens of Jezero City breathed. It also purified the air within the city, filtering out impurities, recycling the buildup of CO and CO_2, and storing the carbon element for industrial use.

These gases were extracted using a multitude of processes: chemical, electrical, and biological. This meant that the entire area had a foul, acrid smell, and was probably the reason why there were no people to be seen anywhere.

Mia and Gizmo eventually moved past this area onto yet another large, circular emergency airlock. It was open, as they all were, and they passed through it into an old and dilapidated industrial sector. They moved along a long, straight causeway that terminated around five hundred meters ahead of them. On either side of this causeway were large industrial units, all of which seemed to be closed up and abandoned. This was a sector that had suffered greatly during the Great Storm and had never recovered.

"Perfect place to hide a bio-lab," Mia said as she glanced around the area. It was at the very western edge of the city and stuck out like a finger from the city perimeter. This was designed to facilitate rover traffic to dock with the units. This meant that each one had its own surface airlock, perfect for smuggling goods in and out of Jezero.

The lighting was dim, and a thin haze seemed to permeate the air as if the filters in this sector no longer worked. "I thought you said the air was clean here." Mia glanced up at the curved roof. "Wouldn't surprise me if the entire place is losing atmosphere."

"I said the APU sector was. We have just passed that." Gizmo pointed ahead. "This way, it is just up here."

Finally, they came to a halt outside a wide entrance door to a gray, nondescript unit. There was no indication anywhere as to what its purpose might be, or might have been in the past.

"Are you sure this is it?"

"Are you seriously asking me that question?" Gizmo replied as it set about dismantling the door control panel.

Mia didn't reply. Instead she took out her plasma weapon, checked it, and held it in both hands, ready for whatever might be behind that door. "This place looks pretty beat up. I hope it still retains a pressurized atmosphere."

"It does," Gizmo said as the door clicked, then whirred, then rose up.

Mia kept her back to the side wall until it was high enough to crouch under. The space was dark, dusty, and deserted.

Gizmo flicked on its light and swept it around the area. Not only was it deserted, it was completely empty except for some scraps of packaging that lay strewn on the ground.

"Let's check in there." Mia jerked her head in the direction of the offices attached to the unit.

Gizmo again dismantled the door control panel and gained access. Again, this area was empty and deserted.

"Nothing," Mia said. "Not a single goddamn thing." She put her back against a wall and slumped down on the floor. "I don't believe this. I was sure this was it." She shook her head. "If we don't find this pathogen soon, then the population is done for."

"We could check the exterior airlock. That has quite a volume. One could hide a considerable amount of equipment in there."

Mia perked up. "Of course. Gizmo, you're a genius."

"I know."

They headed back out across the main floor area and over to the airlock at the rear of the unit. Mia kept the PEP weapon at the ready, her back to the wall as Gizmo hit the button to open the interior door. Mia wasn't taking any chances. It may be that someone was here and decided to hide in the airlock; unlikely, but best to be prepared.

The door split in the center with a slight hiss, and both sides retracted into the side walls, exposing a large, empty space.

Mia sighed and lowered her weapon. "Nothing." She sat down on the floor again. "Well, that's it, Gizmo. I'm all out of ideas. Nowhere else to look. And even if there was, we're probably too late."

"Do not give up hope just yet. The entire Jezero City security services are actively searching for it. They may get lucky."

"And what is the probability of that?"

"Difficult to say with any accuracy. But my best guess would be less than 1%."

26

BREAKDOWN

Jann kept watch at the doorway to the network room while Nills contacted Capt. Aby to give her the details on the tunnel along with the strength of the Xenonists' defensive position. Xenon stood alongside her, and she could feel the tension radiating off his body like an electrical charge. He was edgy, wound up tight, ready to bolt off again. She really hoped he wasn't going to do anything reckless. At least, no more reckless than what they were already doing.

Jann's thoughts shifted to the cloning cavern with its rows and rows of tanks disappearing off into the darkness. *How has it come to this?* she thought. *To have created a clone army without a single person in the Council knowing about it. Someone had to have known. It just wasn't possible to keep all this secret. But maybe they didn't think it would escalate all the way up to Argon's genocidal finale. Too late now,* she concluded. *Unless the release site in Jezero could be found in time, then...*

"Done." Nills' voice broke through Jann's thoughts. "And two more MLOD transports are on their way. They'll be here soon, and Aby says once they land they will storm the enclave."

"Okay, good." Jann nodded and turned to go, but Xenon stopped her.

"You don't have to come with me," Xenon said, looking from her to Nills and back. "This is something I have to do, something I should have done a long time ago. You stay here, hide out until the MLOD break through."

"Not a chance," Jann said, casting a glance at Nills.

"Sorry, Xenon. Looks like we're all going down together," Nills said with a grin. "Lead the way."

Again, Xenon's intimate knowledge of the facility, with its multitude of passages and stairways, enabled them to move fast, without detection. He finally brought them up a narrow stairwell that opened out into a large industrial pump room, where the irrigation system for the primary dome was operated. It was dark and humid with a dank smell. It hummed and gurgled with the sound of a myriad of motors pumping water through a labyrinth of pipes.

Xenon moved in behind a large cylindrical water tank and gestured for Jann and Nills to follow. He pointed ahead, down toward the far end of the room. "Just up there is a service door leading into the primary dome. It brings us out around a meter below floor level into a kind of stairwell, so it has good cover. To the left is a short set of steps that leads to the floor level, very close to the entrance to the viewing chamber. There'll probably be guards there."

Jann nodded and pulled the plasma weapon out from her waistband, as did Nills. They slowly made their way through the pump room, all the time scanning the area for any workers that might be hidden behind some tank or other. They had just reached at the door when they heard, and felt, an explosion from somewhere deep within the complex.

"They've started the assault. We better hurry before the fight comes to us," said Jann.

Xenon grabbed the door handle and gently opened it, peering through the crack as he did. "All clear," he whispered, and they moved out into the lush, verdant biodome.

They were well concealed in the low stairwell, with thick vegetation all around. Xenon was about to head up the short steps when Jann grabbed his arm. "Wait," she whispered. "Better let myself and Nills take care of the guards. Stay here until I give you the all clear. Okay?" Jann poked a finger at Xenon. "And don't go doing anything stupid."

Xenon hesitated for a beat, then screwed his mouth up and gave her a curt nod, stepping aside to let her and Nills pass.

Jann kept low as she moved up the steps. Her view of

the entrance was obscured by dense foliage, so she reached out with her free hand and pushed back a large leaf to get a better view. Nills moved up to crouch beside her.

"Doors to the viewing chamber are open," she whispered. "Two guards outside. Both sitting, looking bored. That's all I can see."

Nills inched his way forward and snatched a look. "Okay, I'll take the one on the right. Nice and quiet. Let's try not to alert anyone in the area beyond."

They stealthily picked their way through the dense vegetation, keeping low and out of sight. Nills took a route to the right, Jann to the left. She finally arrived at a point well within range of her plasma weapon and scanned the foliage for any sign of Nills. He popped his head out from behind a tall, leafy bush some distance away and signaled that he was ready.

Jann dialed her weapon up a notch or two from stun, nodded to Nills, then took aim and fired. She wasn't taking any chances, wanting to make sure her target would go down and stay down.

The blast slammed into the back of the guard's head, spinning him around, and he collapsed face-down on the dais. His comrade made the mistake of standing up instead of hitting the floor, and Nills' shot hit him square in the back. He too went spinning, and collapsed on top of his buddy.

It was then that Jann heard more plasma weapon fire, coming from the far end of the dome. The MLOD forces were almost here. But before either she or Nills had moved out of their position, Xenon came running up the central path and bounded onto the dais. *Shit*, thought Jann. *He's going in there alone. He'll just get himself killed.*

Yet before he had taken more than a step on the dais, a massive explosion detonated inside the chamber, flinging a cloud of smoke and debris back out into the dome, and sending Xenon tumbling down the path.

"Noooo..." Jann screamed, as she stood up and rushed to the dais. Nills had also emerged from cover and was tending to Xenon.

"Goddammit," Jann shouted back at him. "I think they just blew themselves up, rather than be taken."

A decompression alert started squawking, and the isolation door began to close across the entrance to the viewing chamber, sealing it off. The explosion must have damaged the structure, and it was now losing atmosphere. Any hope Jann had of finding someone alive in there, someone who knew the location of the release site, was fading fast.

She ran toward the closing door, but felt a strong hand grab her arm and haul her back.

"It's too late, Jann," said Nills as his grip tightened. "You'll just get yourself trapped in there."

He was right, of course. And slowly Jann felt the fight drain away, only to be replaced by the realization of defeat. Any hope she had of finding the location lay dying on the floor of the chamber. She slumped down on her knees and buried her head in her hands. All around her the sound of battle raged, weapons fire, shouts, and the squawk of the decompression klaxon. She felt Nills' arms wrap around her shoulders. "We can't stay here. Too dangerous, gotta move. Come on." He tugged at her, she stood up, and allowed him to guide her down from the dais and into the cover of the service stairwell.

"We blew it, Nills. Mars is done for. Everything we've ever fought for is now all for nothing."

"No, I won't believe that. There is still hope, Jann. The MLOD in Jezero are searching every nook and cranny, they may yet find it. There is still hope."

27

APU

"We've failed, Gizmo," Mia said, sitting on the floor of the empty industrial unit with her back to the wall, her knees up under her chin.

"There is still time," Gizmo offered.

"No, Gizmo. There isn't. At least not enough." Mia stood up and kicked an empty crate in frustration. "Dammit. I was sure this was it."

Mia stood still for a moment and stared down at the floor of the unit. The crate had moved slightly and exposed one corner of what looked liked a hatch. "Gizmo, come over here and give me a hand moving this."

Between them they pushed the crate off to one side, revealing a square, airtight hatch, wide enough for a large human to fit through.

Gizmo examined it. "Interesting," it said as it reached

down and turned the recessed handle. The hatch cracked open.

A crudely dug shaft descended approximately five meters down, with a ladder attached to one side. The droid scanned the interior. "Most irregular. I have no record of this on any official Jezero City schematic I possess."

Mia pulled out her plasma weapon again. "Irregular is good, Gizmo. Irregular is what we're looking for." She began to climb down the ladder. The droid followed.

At the base, a horizontal shaft opened up, tall enough for a person to pass through by stooping down a little.

"Perhaps I should take the lead," suggested Gizmo, flipping on its light.

"After you." Mia gestured with a free hand, and they moved off down the tunnel.

It ran in a straight line for around a hundred meters and had clearly been hastily dug. The walls were rough-hewn, with the roof supported by standard extruded beams used in mining. Along the sides, automatic lighting had been hastily rigged. The floor was flat but dusty, which got kicked up by Gizmo's tracks. Mia pulled her scarf over her mouth; exposure to raw Martian regolith came with a health warning. There were a lot of compounds in it that were dangerous to breathe in over a prolonged period.

The tunnel finally came to an end, with another short vertical shaft leading upward. A ladder ascended along one side to another hatch, similar to one they had entered through. Mia climbed up, turned the locking wheel, and pushed it open a little. There was a slight hiss as she did, indicating a pressure differential.

The first thing to assault her senses was the noise of machines, and then a chill hit her face. The air was dry and caught in her throat, and she coughed. She could see a large industrial area, forested by pipes and ducting, but no people. She opened the hatch fully and climbed out, quickly followed by Gizmo.

"What is this place?" Mia asked as they extracted themselves from the shaft.

"It is a section of the atmosphere processing unit. This area pumps clean recycled air back into this sector of the city."

"Good place to release a pathogen," said Mia as she stood up and began to look around. The space was cavernous, with a high ceiling, yet it was packed with indefinable industrial units all interconnected with a myriad of ducts and pipes.

"We'll never find anything in here." Mia glanced around, trying to find something, anything that would give her a clue. Then she looked down and spotted a faint trail of dusty footprints leading out from the hatch.

"Gizmo, look here." She crouched down and ran a finger through the dust. "They've left us a trail." Mia then froze. "Shit. You hear that? Someone's talking."

"I sense two distinct voice patterns, approximately

three point four meters in that direction." Gizmo pointed dead ahead.

"They could just be workers. They might even help us."

"It is possible, even probable."

"Come, let's follow these footprints. Keep quiet, and try to eyeball the owners of those voices before they see us, just in case."

"A wise precaution, Mia."

They treaded their way through a gap in the machinery, but the trail disappeared. This area had higher foot traffic, and so the footprints had been eradicated. Gizmo scanned the floor and pointed to another tight gap between two large units. "Over there." They picked up the trail and squeezed themselves through.

The footprints ended again. Not because they were erased, but because this was the final destination. A large air duct, mounted at head height, bisected the area.

"Air outflow duct," Gizmo informed as it ran its light along the underside.

Mia did the same with hers, moving in the opposite direction. "Gizmo," she whispered, "I think I may have found something."

Strapped to the underside of the wide metal duct was a silver metal canister around the size of a fire extinguisher. Attached to that was an assemblage of exposed electronics, twisted pipes, and a small, old-fashioned digital display. Mia leaned in and blew the dust off its face. Several groups of numerical data were displayed, but the one that stood out was a timer, counting down: 9:47, 9:46, 9:45...

"I would not interfere with that if I were you," Gizmo said as it lowered itself into a position where it could scan the apparatus.

"Can you stop it, disassemble it in some way?"

The droid twitched a little as it analyzed. "Anti-tamper device. See here." The droid pointed at a section of electronics, but it all looked the same to Mia.

"I'll take your word on it. So how do we stop it?"

"The gas discharge is attached to the duct here, via this pipe. I should be able to bypass the tamper switch, then I can remove it from the duct. But it will still be active."

"Could we bring it outside, onto the surface? It would be harmless in the Martian atmosphere."

"8:35. I concur. With the time remaining, that is our best option."

Mia shuffled out of the way and let Gizmo get to work.

The droid took its time, carefully analyzing the makeup and arrangement of the device, to the point where Mia was about to tell it to hurry up. She became so wound up that she didn't hear the two guards approaching until one shouted out. "Hey, what are you doing there?"

Mia turned around, raised her hands, and walked out toward them. "This is a critical emergency. Get a message to the MLOD and tell them we have found the pathogen release site."

One of the guards jerked his weapon at Gizmo. "Tell your droid to stop what it's doing and move away."

"You don't understand, the entire population of Jezero, and Mars, is at stake here."

"I said move it, this is your last warning." He raised his weapon while the other guard talked into his cuff. *"Need some backup here. They've located the device."*

Xenonists, thought Mia. *Goddammit, they must be everywhere.* She took her chance and dived behind a large fan unit as a plasma blast sailed past her head. She paused for a beat, pressed herself up against the unit, and returned fire. But it was wild. Just random blasts, as she couldn't see where she was aiming. Yet a scream told her she had hit one of them. She chanced a quick glance around the side of the unit. One guard was down, the other was nowhere to be seen.

"Gizmo, you'd better get a move on. We'll have a load of these guys on us any second."

"I have deactivated the tamper mechanism and disconnected the air flow feed. But I estimate five more minutes are required to disable the activation system."

"We don't have five minutes, we've got seconds."

The droid extracted itself from beneath the air duct carrying the entire apparatus. "Then our only option is to get it outside via the external airlock back in the industrial unit. We have time to make that."

"Okay, but stay behind me." Mia shuffled forward and stuck her head around a set of vertical pipes to scan the area. A plasma blast sailed toward her from her right-hand side. She ducked back just in time.

"Looks like just one guard so far, over that way, around ten meters away." She jerked a thumb over her shoulder. "Get ready to dash across. I'll give you cover."

She reached out and started firing in the general direction of the other guard. "Go, go."

Gizmo sped across the gap and disappeared in through a maze of machinery. Mia kept firing and followed the droid. She made it in through the gap, but in the corner of her eye she saw several more guards running up toward them.

"There's more coming, hurry," Mia shouted down as she arrived at the hatch. Gizmo was already inside, speeding away. Mia dropped down, closed the hatch, and spun the locking wheel. She considered jamming something into it, but there was no time to think. She dropped down onto the floor and ran down the tunnel.

Ahead, at the far end, Gizmo had stopped at the base of the ladder. "What are you waiting for?" she shouted. "Go, go."

"I cannot climb the ladder and hold this apparatus at the same time."

"What?"

"Unlike you, I do not possess legs. I require both arms to haul myself up."

"Goddammit." Mia could hear the other hatch being opened. "Give it to me. Quick," she shouted.

Gizmo handed her the unit, then clambered up. Once up top, Mia threw the unit to the droid, then started up the ladder. She had only gone a few rungs when a plasma blast slammed into the sidewall behind her, sending dust and rock flying in all directions. A second blast hit the wall just centimeters from her hip, but it was enough to send a spasm of electrically charged energy coursing through her body. She screamed out in pain and lost her footing, hanging onto the ladder by just one hand.

Gizmo looked over the opening and reached down.

"Leave me," Mia shouted. "Get that out to the surface."

But the droid ignored her, instead grabbing her wrist and hauling her up as two more blasts hit the ladder beneath her.

"We are already out of time, Mia. I will not be able to cycle through the external airlock. But there is another option."

Mia struggled to think of what that might be. The pain in her upper body was excruciating. At the same time, her lower body was beginning to go numb; she was losing the ability to use her legs.

"My apologies in advance, Mia. But you have a slim chance of surviving."

"What?"

"The airlock. It is your only chance." With that, the droid picked her up and flung her across the area with as much momentum as it could. Mia sailed through the air, hit the floor hard, and tumbled into the open airlock. She finally came to a stop when she slammed into the outer door.

Mia lifted her head up to see several guards piling out of the tunnel, taking aim at Gizmo, who was racing across the space at high speed. Then she realized what it had meant by *another option*. It wasn't planning on using the exterior airlock, it was just going to drive straight through the outer wall of the unit.

"Oh shit."

Mia crawled across to the side of the airlock, grabbed the handrail, and threaded her arm around it just as the droid smashed through the end wall and out onto the Martian surface.

The hole it left began to rapidly widen, with the sides being torn off by the pressure of air being evacuated. One of the guards clung onto the edge of the hatch while two others began to be sucked out. They clawed the floor, looking for any purchase.

Mia shimmied along the handrail and tried to reach the control panel to activate the door. She strained and stretched as she began to feel the pull on her body. She was being lifted off the ground.

With one final effort, she stabbed at the button and the doors began to close. The evacuating air began to pull at her until she was almost horizontal, and the pain in her elbow joint became almost unbearable—it was the only thing keeping her from being sucked out. The doors continued their achingly slow closure as Mia felt her lungs beginning to struggle for air. Every fiber of her body screamed in pain. Her head swam, her strength began to fail, and finally she blacked out.

EPILOGUE

A sleek, state-owned transport shuttle gracefully lifted off from its pad on the outskirts of Jezero City, slowly rising up into the early morning Martian sun. As it ascended, it rotated to orient itself on the correct transit vector, then moved forward, slowly at first, but picking up speed as it passed over the crater rim.

On board, Dr. Jann Malbec sat in a well-appointed passenger seat and gazed out the side window at the landscape. The shuttle flew low, skirting the peak of the crater rim. The air was clear, and the sun still low over the east, casting long, early morning shadows across the dunes below. The outer edge of the craggy peaks of Jezero Crater swooped down into the Isidis Basin, morphing into low, undulating sand dunes that carried on for as far as her eye could see. The shuttle banked, orienting itself for a direct flight to its ultimate destination, the former enclave of Xenon Hybrid.

ARGON WAS DEAD, as were many of his followers. The battle that had raged for control of the enclave had been brutal, as the Xenonists fought with typical ideological zeal, preferring to die defending the facility rather than surrender. Even though they greatly outnumbered the MLOD forces, they were no match for the battle droids and attack drones utilized by highly skilled operatives.

Yet in the aftermath, many of those who survived felt they had been betrayed. Few of the foot soldiers within the cult knew of the plot to release a pathogen to exterminate all but those with enhanced DNA. Apart from Argon, only a handful, less than twenty, were in on it. For the others, the revelation came as a shock. Most were initially in denial, then came revulsion, then anger that their trust and belief had been so heinously violated. Yet there were others who, while not condoning the action, were sympathetic to the principle.

For the Martian state, the problem was what to do with these extremists. The surviving ringleaders were tried and subsequently incarcerated. But it was not practically possible for the fledging state to lock up over one hundred and fifty followers of the cult. And some of these very disciples had now become so angry that they began to argue for governmental reforms, so that no group could be hoodwinked in this manner ever again. Ironically, far from seeking the demise of the Martian state, they now advocated for its enhancement.

But the most seismic repercussion was how the entire episode affected the general citizenry. Shock was an understatement. It seemed that the population had entered into a daze. The audacity of the plot was almost too much for people to fathom, and so for quite a while they simply did not know what to think, nor how to react. It was as if the people of Mars were suffering from a collective post-traumatic stress disorder. Not surprising, considering they had just come through a rebel revolt in Syrtis along with the worst sand storm ever recorded on Mars, and now this. Something needed to be done to lift the population out of its collective funk.

"Dr. Malbec?" the flight steward called over from the flight deck companionway. "The captain wants you to know that we'll be arriving in twenty minutes. Also, she's just received a message that all the other delegates have arrived."

Jann nodded. "Okay, thanks." She then went back to staring out the side window at the flat, barren landscape rushing past beneath the craft.

THE OTHER PROBLEM, of course, was what to do with the head-of-state position. Xenon had abdicated, feeling that he had ultimately done the office a disservice, that the title that was bestowed on him only served to award him an unwanted cult following—one that was all too easy to infiltrate and corrupt.

Therefore, who should be next? Should there even be a head-of-state? All these questions and more were now considered of critical importance for the future of the Martian population, and so they entered a long period of soul searching. If the society were to survive and prosper on Mars, then they needed to get their act together and give some serious consideration on how it was to be governed.

Their current system of ad hoc arrangements, tacit agreements, unwritten rules, and corporate contracts was no longer sustainable. A much more formal system was needed, one that would allow for some modicum of political and social stability.

The irony, in Jann's mind, was that while humanity's technical brilliance enabled people to live and work on another planet, they still struggled when it came to the messy business of governance. There was no AI that could be applied. No grand computer that could make these decisions. No algorithm that took its inputs from all parties, vested interests, social needs, security concerns, and disparate cultures—and then spit out an elegant solution.

In that sense, Mars was no different than all past human civilizations that struggled to govern themselves. Any injustices, perceived or otherwise, if left unchecked soon developed into agitation, protest, insurrection, revolution, chaos, and ultimately collapse. Yet for some, those societies that bring themselves to the very edge of the abyss and glimpse the horror of their future pull back from the brink before it's too late. After which, a long period of soul-searching begins. And this was the point at which the society on Mars had finally arrived. To go forward, a new paradigm was needed, one that offered a future free from strife.

Yet, no one was under any illusions that this would be an easy task. Where, in the entire history of humanity, had it ever been? But it was not impossible, and most agreed that it was absolutely necessary. So, after a period of acrimonious discussion between the representatives of the multitude of interests on Mars, it was agreed that the current ruling council would be moved out of Jezero City to a more neutral location. The process of selecting councilors would also be reorganized, to better represent the patchwork quilt of people and interests that existed on Mars. But where was this neutral place?

In the end, a radical solution was proposed. The old enclave of Xenon Hybrid would be repurposed. It was big enough and far enough away as not to be seen as aligned to any of the primary population centers of Jezero, Syrtis, or Elysium. It was also the site of one of the earliest research outposts, therefore its history could be traced back all the way to the foundation. So, the old bio-labs and cloning tanks were ripped out and destroyed, and a new administration facility built in its place.

Overseeing this, as well as the installation of a state-of-the-art AI to manage the life support, was Nills and his team, assisted in no small part by Gizmo, who had now become almost an appendage to Langthorp. They were seldom seen apart, and Nills had become borderline obsessed with protecting the droid, and would countenance no discussion around its future other than the one he had envisaged for it. But no one really argued with him. After all, the droid had become a national treasure, and whatever Langthorp wanted was okay with everyone else. Including Jann, and Mia for that matter.

The shuttle banked again, and the outline of the enclave came into view through the starboard window where Jann sat. She could see where new additions to the facility had been made, including a new shuttle port, already packed full of craft as people assembled for the inauguration ceremony. She took her eyes away from the vista and looked across the interior of the craft to where Mia Sorelli sat, in the seat opposite. Mia was looking straight ahead, deep in thought.

"You okay?" Jann said over the noise of the engines that were changing tempo for a landing.

"Yeah, fine," Mia said as she shifted in her seat. "But you know how I hate these...ceremonies."

"Three sols. It's going to be a long one. But you don't have to stay for it all, just your part."

"I don't see why they're giving me this medal. It seems so...unnecessary."

"Every society has its rituals, Mia. They signal the

value system. It matters—and let's face it, you're a hero. Someone deserving of this accolade."

"I don't know. I just did what I had to do, nothing more. And really, it should be Gizmo getting this accolade."

"Perhaps, but I'm not sure we're ready as a society to elevate droids to such an exalted position."

"I'm not making a speech, I told them that. They can give me the medal up on the podium, but that's it." Mia shifted again in her seat, then rubbed her right thigh.

"How's your back?"

"I still get a twinge down my side from time to time. Which is fine. For a while there I didn't think I'd walk again. So, I can live with a bit of discomfort."

"Can I get you something for it?" Zack leaned out from his seat, his face eager to execute his new duties as aide to Envoy Sorelli. He had made a full recovery, and when word got out in the MLOD that the position of assistant to the envoy was available, he jumped at the opportunity. In the end, it was Mia herself that insisted he get the job. A more suspicious part of Jann's mind considered that maybe there was more there than simply mutual respect. But she would leave that speculation to the social commentators.

"I'm going to stay for the full event, by the way. I can't miss your inauguration. Although, I don't think you can get away without making a speech."

"Thanks, I need all the moral support I can get. It can get lonely up there on the pedestal."

"You'll make a great head-of-state, a real one this time. Having Xenon was a mistake, he was just too weird. Didn't take it seriously."

"He did in his own way, I suppose. Xenon was a philosopher. He saw it more as a passive symbol of our unique culture rather than something civic. But who's to say he won't take the office again sometime in the future? Seeing as how his genetic profile indicates he could live to be two hundred."

They were silent for a moment before Mia spoke again. "Nervous?"

"About taking it on?"

"Yeah. You know, it's a lot of responsibility."

"I'll be honest, Mia, I hesitated when it was first mooted. Why me? Surely there were others more worthy."

"Nonsense, Jann. You go all the way back, almost to the beginning. You brought independence, prosperity, and have seen off multiple plots to undermine the colony. So if not you, then who? No one else fits that bill. You are the best person to represent this new era we're entering into."

"I appreciate the moral support, Mia. And you're right, we are entering a new chapter on this planet. Hopefully one where the only law on Mars is *no longer your own.*"

THE END

. . .

I HOPE you enjoyed reading this story as much as I enjoyed writing it for you. If you did, then please leave me a review. Just a simple 'liked it' would be great, it helps a lot.

ALSO BY GERALD M. KILBY

Why not check out my other series, The Belt.

Out in the asteroid belt, you're never far from a rock and a hard place.

Commander Scott McNabb and the crew of the science vessel, Hermes, are three years into a five-year-long survey of the asteroid belt when they discover a derelict spaceship in orbit around a binary asteroid. The ship contains an experimental quantum device, lost while en route to a research colony on Europa.

Yet once word of the crew's discovery gets out, they soon realize that ownership of this technology could fundamentally change the balance of power within the colonized worlds, and they now find themselves at the very nexus of a system-wide conflict.

ABOUT THE AUTHOR

Gerald M. Kilby grew up on a diet of Isaac Asimov, Arthur C. Clark, and Frank Herbert, which developed into a taste for Iain M. Banks and everything ever written by Neal Stephenson. Understandable then, that he should choose science fiction as his weapon of choice when entering the fray of storytelling.

CHAIN REACTION is his first novel and is very much in the old-school techno-thriller style while his latest books, **COLONY MARS** and **THE BELT,** are both best sellers, topping Amazon charts for Hard Science Fiction and Space Exploration.

He lives in the city of Dublin, Ireland, in the same neighborhood as Bram Stoker and can be sometimes seen tapping away on a laptop in the local cafe with his dog Loki.

You can connect with Gerald M. Kilby at:
www.geraldmkilby.com